Fairytale Brides

Once upon a proposal...

Opening the Happy Ever After Agency is a dream come true for coowners Harriet, Emilia, Alexandra and Amber. London's newest bespoke concierge service offers clients everything they could possibly wish for!

Their professional lives are finally on track, but their personal lives are about to be turned upside down...by four handsome men, who will whisk them away to every corner of the globe, and present them with the proposals of a lifetime!

Discover Harriet's story in

Honeymooning with Her Brazilian Boss

Available now!

And look out for Emilia, Alexandra and Amber's stories

Coming soon!

Dear Reader,

Before I knew anything else about this book, I knew I wanted a Brazilian hero, part inspired by Thiago Soares, principal at The Royal Ballet, and part inspired by a country very, very high on my "places I want to visit next, please" list. I also knew I wanted to write a series about four friends, each one loosely based on a fairy tale.

Both Harriet and Deangelo are lonely, and the losses in their pasts have set them apart, so they find it easier to watch from the sidelines. When Deangelo gets the opportunity to right a historic wrong he needs his ex-PA's help—but soon finds that posing as honeymooners is a very different proposition to working together in the safe confines of an office!

I absolutely adored bringing Deangelo and Harriet to life and creating the Happy Ever After Agency. I hope you love it, too.

Love

Jessica x

Honeymooning with Her Brazilian Boss

Jessica Gilmore

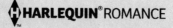

HARLEQUIN® ROMANCE

**Recycling programs
for this product may
not exist in your area.**

ISBN-13: 978-1-335-49931-8

Honeymooning with Her Brazilian Boss

First North American publication 2019

Copyright © 2019 by Jessica Gilmore

This edition published by arrangement with Harlequin Books S.A.

For questions and comments about the quality of this book,
please contact us at CustomerService@Harlequin.com.

® and TM are trademarks of Harlequin Enterprises Limited or its
corporate affiliates. Trademarks indicated with ® are registered in the
United States Patent and Trademark Office, the Canadian Intellectual
Property Office and in other countries.

Printed in U.S.A.

A former au pair, bookseller, marketing manager and seafront trader, **Jessica Gilmore** now works for an environmental charity in York, England. Married with one daughter, one fluffy dog and two dog-loathing cats, she spends her time avoiding housework and can usually be found with her nose in a book. Jessica writes emotional romance with a hint of humor, a splash of sunshine and a great deal of delicious food—and equally delicious heroes!

Books by Jessica Gilmore

Harlequin Romance

Wedding Island

Baby Surprise for the Spanish Billionaire

Summer at Villa Rosa

A Proposal from the Crown Prince

Maids Under the Mistletoe

Her New Year Baby Secret

The Life Swap

In the Boss's Castle
Unveiling the Bridesmaid

The Sheikh's Pregnant Bride
Summer Romance with the Italian Tycoon

Visit the Author Profile page
at Harlequin.com for more titles.

For Nana and Papa. I wish I didn't know so much about how dementia robs us of loved ones too early, and I wish you had both been spared. I hope you're happy and at peace now xxx

Praise for
Jessica Gilmore

"The story is well developed...the emotions make you feel the story and breathe life into the pages. This is a wonderful love story sure to bring a smile to your heart."

—*Harlequin Junkie* on *Her New Year Baby Secret*

"A fantastic read from a fabulous talent, *Unveiling the Bridesmaid* is another triumph from the immensely gifted pen of Jessica Gilmore!"

—*Goodreads*

CHAPTER ONE

'COME ALONG, HATTY. Leave that!'

Harriet Fairchild looked up from her computer screen, eyes full of spreadsheets and numbers and projections, and smiled at the petite woman jiggling impatiently from foot to foot by the side of the pretty antique desk.

'I just need to finish this and I'll be right there. Five minutes, Amber, I promise.'

'You said that ten minutes ago,' Amber pointed out. 'Our guests will be here in fifteen minutes and we haven't had our private toast yet. Those spreadsheets will still be there in the morning.'

'Along with everything else I haven't managed to do yet. I can't believe I'm so behind, when we haven't even opened the agency.' But Harriet was saving the documents as she spoke, closing down the laptop and shutting the lid with a sigh she did her best to hide from the bubbly redhead. Her new business partners—and best friends—had been more than understanding when Harriet disappeared across London most days to sit with her father after yet another fall, but with the Happy Ever After Agency due to open its doors imminently she knew it should have been all hands on deck back at the elegant Chelsea townhouse where they now lived, worked and dreamed.

'I can't believe it's actually happening.' Amber bounced up and down on her trainer-clad tiptoes as Harriet slipped her laptop into the desk drawer and locked it. 'That we've made it.'

'We're not there yet; we need some clients first.' But although Harriet was trying to maintain her usual calm and sensible manner, excitement fizzed inside her like the champagne Emilia was getting ready to uncork on the other side of the room.

'Well, that's what tonight's about. Launching the business. After tonight we'll have more work than we can cope with, you'll see.'

'We will if the other two have anything to do with it. Between Emilia's event skills and Alex's PR skills, how can our launch event be anything but a success? And if it isn't, well, we can live off canapés and champagne for the next week!'

She followed Amber through the office and into the freshly decorated reception area, where the other two co-owners of the Happy Ever After Agency were waiting for her. As she joined them Emilia finally let the cork go with a resounding pop, Alexandra deftly holding a glass under the bottle to catch the first rush of golden bubbles, handing the filled glass to Harriet with a smile.

'Thank you!' Harriet took the glass and held it out, waiting till the other three each held their own to join her in the toast. 'To dreams coming true and happy-ever-afters,' she said.

'To happy-ever-afters,' Emilia echoed, her answering smile for once full and frank, the shadows that usually haunted her eyes nowhere to be seen.

'And to all our dreams.' Alexandra could never be anything but cool and collected, but her even, polite smile was genuinely warm, the excitement in her voice unfeigned.

'To us.' Amber was never less than sunny and her smile lit up the room. 'We've done it. I'm so proud of us!'

Harriet turned to Alexandra, her heart full of gratitude. 'And earlier than planned, thanks to you, Alex.'

The tall, slim girl shook her immaculately coiffed head. 'Thanks to my godmother, you mean. She left me this place. Without her, our dreams would still be just that, only dreams.'

'To your fairy godmother, then.' Amber raised her glass in another toast and the small group responded with a respectful murmur. They all knew how lucky they were. Alexandra's inheritance meant that not only were they opening the agency a couple of years earlier than planned, they didn't have to worry about renting premises or any of the overhead costs starting a new business usually entailed.

Harriet took a sip of the champagne, trying to work out just what it was that made this vintage twenty times more expensive than her usual brand of corner shop Prosecco, and looked around the room, unable to stop herself critically surveying it, looking for flaws or potential problems. Her stomach settled, the squeeze in her chest relaxing as she saw nothing out of place. They were ready, and after tonight's launch the great, good and wealthy of Chelsea would know that they were here and that they were open for business.

Luckily the small Chelsea townhouse Alexandra had inherited was structurally perfect, if outdated in decor, but between them they had saved just enough to knock down the wall between the front sitting room and back dining room to create the light, inviting reception and office space they now stood in. Wooden floorboards shone with a warm golden glow, the replastered walls were freshly painted matt white above the picture rails and a light grey below and the original tiled fireplaces had been scrubbed until they shone. Two comfortable-looking sofas sat opposite each other at the front of the room, inviting spaces for potential clients or staff to relax in, and their own desks, an eclectic mixture of vintage and modern classic, faced the reception area in two rows, paperwork neatly filed in the shelves built into the alcoves by the back fireplace. Flowers and plants softened the space, a warm floral print on the blinds and curtains, the same theme picked up in the pictures hanging on the walls. They wanted their public-facing space to look professional and yet unique. Like the services they offered.

The door at the back led to a narrow kitchen and a sunny conservatory extension they used as a sitting/dining room. Usually the door would remain closed, keeping the area private, but today it was flung open to welcome their new neighbours and potential clients to their launch party, the fridge filled with a much less expensive champagne than the one they were currently drinking, the tables and counters covered with an array of tempting canapés baked by Amber over the last two days. The scent of warm spices and fresh bread mingled aromatically with the beeswax polish and fresh flowers.

Upstairs, each of the two floors housed two bedrooms and a bathroom. Thanks to Alexandra's generosity, this was all theirs. The bills were to be paid out of the agency profits, each partner only drawing enough salary for simple needs, the rest to be pooled back in until they had enough for what each of them truly dreamed for—security. Security and a home. Harriet inhaled, letting the unique scent fill her lungs. Security, home and a family.

'Ten minutes, girls.' Emilia brought Harriet back to the here and now. 'Are we ready?'

'The office couldn't look more perfect,'

Harriet said. 'And we're all looking present-able, too.' She grinned at the understatement. As usual her friends looked stunning; they had agreed to all wear black, and if Harriet's sensible wrap dress looked dull next to Al-ex's elegant shift, Amber's vintage-inspired swing dress and Emilia's pretty floaty skirt and lace top, well, she was more than used to fading into the background. Preferred it in fact.

'I've been chatting up all the neighbours,' Amber said. 'They've all been invited per-sonally and I managed a subtle sales pitch at the same time. I've identified several in need of an emergency childcare provider, dog walkers and housekeeping and I've already been approached for some light cleaning and shopping for a couple of elderly residents I spoke to in the park. And while chatting I made sure they know that I have all the con-tacts. I reckon we'll hear from some time-poor, cash-rich families wanting their date nights organised from babysitters to impos-sible-to-get-into restaurants before the week is out…' Amber specialised in providing be-spoke concierge services. At Aion, the com-pany they had all recently left, her role had been to run the small team who ensured VIP clients wanted or needed for nothing, no matter how short the notice.

'And I've already got a couple of events lined up and the clients are, of course, invited tonight. First up a charity brunch and then two birthdays; one is for a child, Amber, so maybe we can combine on that? Children are definitely more your thing than mine.' Emilia smiled over at her friend. 'I can't wait to get going. If we can pull these off then we might have a chance at some of the Christmas balls, and they will really get our reputation out there.'

'There's a new restaurant opening up the street and I have offered to do their PR. It doesn't pay much but it's a nice story for our launch.' Alexandra was all about the story. Even after four years Harriet wasn't sure what was real and what was manufactured about her friend, but it didn't matter. The truth was they were four kindred spirits, four lonely souls who had found each other one Christmas Eve and slowly formed a semblance of a family.

'I have temps coming in to interview all week,' Harriet contributed. 'I had hoped to be further along by now but…'

'But nothing. We have the time and space

to build the agency up carefully and properly. The right staff, the right clients and the best service,' Alex reassured her. 'We're in this for the long-term. Your dad is important, Harriet, more important than anything else. Never apologise for being with him.'

'Thank you.' Harriet's whole body warmed with affection and relief. She didn't have to make excuses here, hide her emotions and needs. She belonged. It was all she had ever wanted. 'Hang on, was that the bell? It sounds like our first guests have arrived...'

Deangelo Santos didn't often read magazines. He certainly didn't read gossip magazines. And since the day he'd first set foot on British soil, twelve years before, all his reading material had been in English. The bright, gaudy Brazilian magazine lying on his desk was as out of place in his severely modern and austere office as a child's teddy bear. But he hadn't bought the magazine to read it. He'd bought it to allow himself one glorious moment of anticipation.

Three faces smiled out of the front cover. All in their forties, all sleek and self-satisfied in the way that only inherited privilege and extreme arrogance could instil. And all completely unaware that in just a few weeks their entire lives would be turned upside down, inside out and ripped apart. Deangelo allowed himself just one moment of looking at the magazine, the faintest semblance of a smile curling his lips, before picking it up between his thumb and forefinger and tossing it into the recycling bin. He stalked to his office door. It was time to put the final pieces of his plan into play.

He threw open the glass door and stifled a sigh as the slight woman who occupied the desk outside jumped. It was a tiny jump, almost imperceptible, but there all the same. 'Good evening, Mr Santos. Is there anything I can do for you before I leave?'

There was nothing wrong with the question or the way she asked it. Just as there was nothing wrong with her work. For the last two weeks she had been sitting at this very desk when he arrived at work at seven thirty a.m. after his usual ten kilometre run and half-hour workout. He would walk into his office to find his computer switched on and waiting for him, his task list neatly printed out and waiting on his keyboard, the bitter dark coffee he preferred brewed and waiting. Everything as it should be.

Equally she had been right there, at her desk all day, taking less than half an hour for lunch, managing his inbox and diary, booking flights and arranging meetings, making sure he was only disturbed when he needed to be.

Just as he liked it.

Now here she still was, ten hours after starting, not complaining about her long day or showing impatient signs of wanting to get home.

Although, to be fair, she would be handsomely paid for exactly those kinds of hours.

Really, in the grand scheme of things one small nervous jump wasn't anything to complain about.

Except...

Except it was Monday. Which meant the woman sitting at his PA's desk had been here for two weeks and one day.

And that one extra day was unexpected. Deangelo didn't like unexpected. He planned and schemed and went through every possible contingency to avoid the unexpected. Having your life ripped away from you before you hit your teens would do that to a person.

Instead of answering her question, Deangelo wheeled round and walked back into his office, pulled his phone out of his pocket, pressed a button and waited, foot tapping impatiently until the call was answered.

It took less than three seconds. Good. 'Hello, sir. How can I help?'

'Where is Harriet?' he demanded.

There was a pause before his head of HR responded. 'Harriet?'

'Yes. Harriet. Tall. Blonde hair.' Or was it red? He could never decide. Not that her hair colour mattered, the only thing of any import was that Harriet Fairchild kept his life smooth, in order and seamless. As it should be. 'She's had two weeks off already. When is she due back?'

'Mr Santos, Harriet left.'

'Left?'

'Left the company.'

She had *what*? Deangelo paused, trying to remember the last day he had seen her. Come to think of it, she had looked a little expectant when saying goodbye. Maybe even disappointed? It was hard to remember; he had been putting his final plans together for Brazil that week, his head, for once, nowhere near business as usual.

But how could he have not realised she

was leaving? At least that explained the flowers on her desk…

'Where has she gone? I assume you offered her appropriate recompense to stay?'

'I did, naturally. I know how you dislike your routine changing but she is setting up her own business; I don't think there was any inducement we could have offered to make her stay.' Sue, his head of HR, sounded a lot more sure of herself now and Deangelo couldn't blame her. It was a different matter losing his valued PA to her own business than losing her to another company. Still inconvenient, though. Especially with the biggest deal of his life, if not his career, coming up. A deal he had counted on her help to pull off. Deangelo cast a quick look through the open door at the nervous replacement as she sat typing diligently but unable to shield the worry in her eyes, biting her lip as she pretended not to listen in. No, with those kind of acting skills she wouldn't do at all and it was far too late to train anyone else.

'What kind of business?'

'An agency. She has gone into partnership with three other ex-Aion employees. They are providing an all-round service, I believe, from event management to PA temps, household management to reputation management.'

Deangelo seized upon the one piece of information that was relevant. 'They provide PA temps? Excellent. Then hire her back. For the next month. I'll pay double the going rate.' Everyone had their price and a fledgling agency would be more eager than most for business and income. 'Tell her to make sure her passport is up-to-date; we leave for Rio in two weeks, but I want her back in tomorrow.'

He ended the call and stalked across the office to stand at the full-length windows, staring out at the London skyline beyond. Views like this were worth millions, buildings like the one Aion occupied—occupied and owned—in the heart of South Bank were worth more. He lived right here, in a penthouse apartment, his office took up the floor below, his private gym and swimming pool were in the basement, right next to the garage which housed his beloved collection of vintage sports cars. The rest of the building was a thriving hub of some of the world's leading minds and they all worked for him. He had come a long, long way from the *favela*. But when he set foot in

Rio would he be Deangelo Santos, founder of Aion, tech billionaire, philanthropist or would he revert to the street rat, illegitimate son of one of Rio's oldest families? Discarded and left out like the rubbish they had deemed him.

His hands curled into fists. He had the power now and in two weeks he would show them just who he was. And for that he needed everything to be perfect. He needed Harriet.

As if on cue, his mobile rang. Glancing at the screen before he answered, Deangelo began to relax. Sue with the news of Harriet's return, no doubt.

He answered the call with a curt 'Yes?' then listened to the apologetic voice for a moment, incredulity creeping over him. 'What do you mean, she can't do it?'

'She says she hasn't got time. Give her a week and she'll find you a new replacement for Jenny, although she thinks you should give the poor girl more of a chance—her words not mine—but she's too busy setting up the agency at the moment to take a month away. They only opened today, sir; they're holding their launch party tonight. I was just on my way there now.'

Deangelo stilled. 'Launch party? What's

the address? I'll see you there. I'd better speak to Harriet myself.'

He ended the call, cutting off Sue's polite but clearly panicked protests. If Rio was to go to plan then nothing could go wrong and that included Harriet Fairchild's presence. And if he had to go to Chelsea and persuade her himself then that was exactly what he would do. His gaze stole towards the recycling bin and the gaudy magazine cover peeking out the top. He had a deathbed promise to fulfil and nothing—and no one—was going to stand in his way.

CHAPTER TWO

THE HOUSE WAS pleasantly full, closing in on crowded, a steady stream of curious neighbours, local businesses and carefully selected potential clients passing through to sample Amber's spectacular canapés, have a glass of champagne and toast the Happy Ever After Agency's launch. Harriet had watched Alexandra and Emilia turn on their cool, professional charm, while Amber tempted people with tray after tray of delicious treats, disbelief that it was really happening looping around her stomach. This was it. They existed. Their future was entirely in their hands—it was both thrilling and terrifying. Had they really thought when they'd first come up with the idea that it would actually happen? For so long it had seemed a nice pipe dream, not an actual plan.

No more dreaming. Things had just got serious and for the agency to work they needed clients and fast. This party was just the start. It had to be a success.

Leaning against the wall, Harriet pushed away the misgivings that liked to whisper in her ear; she could be at her desk right now, clocking off for the evening, earning a good salary, pension, benefits—safety. It was time she struck out and dared to do— to be—someone new. No longer the mousy little PA, more part of the office furniture than warm flesh and blood. Of so little significance that after three years Deangelo Santos hadn't even said goodbye. She swallowed. She was a fool to be disappointed by the omission, a fool to care. Just because, occasionally, very occasionally, that keen stare had seemed to see her, seemed to know her, didn't mean the connection she'd imagined was real. She might be a Jane Eyre type but that didn't make him Rochester—which was a good thing. Harriet had never visited Deangelo's penthouse suite but she was pretty sure he didn't keep a wife hidden away there!

Enough. She had clients to woo and impress and moping over her old boss's indifference would help nobody. She smiled even though there was no one there to see it, tilting her chin and pushing her shoulders back. *Fake confidence if you don't feel it* was Amber's mantra. It was one she was going to adopt.

Harriet's own job for the evening was, by choice, greeting guests at the door, handing out brochures and booking in appointments and jobs. Small talk had never been her forte; she much preferred having an actual task to do. Besides, this *was* her job, just as networking and promoting was Alex and Emilia's. She would be managing the office for all four of them as well as recruiting and placing the army of temps she hoped to have in place before too long, providing emergency PA cover herself if necessary. She liked the tidiness of admin work, sorting and solving problems, organising. She liked to be needed.

Outside this house there was nobody who needed her any more, nobody who even noticed her. Somehow, between school and now, she'd turned into the invisible woman. She would never regret the decisions that had taken her to this place. Never regret the years she had spent as her dad's carer, the dates she had turned down, the potential friendships that had never come to fruition, the two fledgling relationships that had never progressed beyond possibility, the university place postponed until she had finally, regretfully withdrawn her application. She had no one but her father, and he had no one but her.

But now his dementia had progressed to a level in which she didn't even exist. So where did that leave her?

Harriet summoned up a smile as a couple of guests passed her on their way out, copies of the agency's promotional brochure in their hands. *Stop being so self-pitying.* She had her friends now—and more. She had a new way forward. Thanks to Alex's inheritance she had a new job, a new home, a new purpose and with it a new resolve: that it was time to stop living on the sidelines, time to step out, actually try living not merely existing. To try and live a life that was more than work and responsibility, now that her father didn't know who she was, now she no longer needed to spend every spare hour by his side. She would start by signing up for the evening language courses and the local book group and see about local volunteering opportunities. Not the wildest activities for someone just turned twenty-six, but a lot wilder than a night in alone with a herbal tea and a book.

And maybe while she was in this spirit she should stop skulking in the hallway with a tablet and a handful of leaflets and go and circulate as the other three were so effortlessly doing. She'd been to many work receptions while she worked at Aion, all over the world. She could do this… Resolutely she turned around but, as she did so, the old-fashioned doorbell rang its sonorous chime.

Pausing, Harriet cast a quick glance in the mirror to make sure she still looked like the professional, aspirational businesswoman stroke hostess that she was trying to be. Okay. Her strawberry-blonde hair hung in a silky sheet, the frizz ruthlessly tamed and controlled, and a discreet coating of lipstick still covered her overly generous mouth. Her wrap dress wasn't gaping and she hadn't spilt anything down it. All that counted as a win. For the umpteenth time in the last two hours Harriet pinned an appropriately pleasant yet professional smile onto her face and opened the door. 'Welcome to…' She looked up before she could complete the sentence and her gaze met a pair of hard amber eyes. She faltered, the door swinging back as she stepped back in shock.

Was she dreaming? Imagining things? Tentatively she reopened the door and looked again. No. No imagining. Tall, broad, the body of a street fighter, face of a fallen angel, marred—or enhanced—by the scar that ran right down one side of his face, temple to chin. A face she knew as well as she knew her own—better, she'd seen it every day for the last three years. 'Deangelo? I mean, Mr Santos, what are you doing here?'

'You're holding a party, aren't you?'

'Erm…yes,' she managed.

'Then aren't you going to invite me in?'

'I…of course.' Harriet was hurriedly running through the many invitations they'd sent and no, she didn't recall the billionaire businessman's name on any of them. Aion's HR staff of course, some of their old colleagues, but not the man himself. He wasn't exactly the party type—and, even after working in close proximity with him, they weren't on invite terms. But, invite or not, Deangelo Santos was not the kind of man to leave cooling his heels on a doorstep, not even a Chelsea doorstep. Besides, she would be mad to turn a man with his money and influence away, and the gleam in his eyes told her he was well aware of the fact. Harriet stood back and nervously, as if she were inviting a predator into her home, said, 'You'd better come in.'

The air seemed to shift as he stepped into the hallway and Harriet was reminded irresistibly of the old vampire movies and the dangers of inviting the powerful over your doorstep. 'Okay, the party is this way. We're actually expecting a few people from Aion.' She smothered a smile at the thought of the shock on their faces when they walked in to see their famously reclusive boss at the party. 'Let me show you around.' She started towards the open partition which linked the hallway to the reception area but Deangelo made no move to follow her.

'Why did you say no?'

Harriet stopped and turned back to face him, startled by the abrupt words. Was *that* why he was here? Surely not. She was a good PA but not that good. 'No? You mean to the temping offer? Because I work here now. It was kind of you to think of me…'

He brushed away her words as if kindness was a foreign concept. 'You are a temp agency. I am in need of a temp. I want to hire you. It makes no sense for you to refuse.'

'But you have a PA. I trained her myself.'

Distaste flickered across Deangelo Santos's face. 'She rustles. And she jumps when I speak.'

'She *rustles*?' Harriet blinked. Maybe she had fallen asleep at her desk and this was some kind of surreal dream. It wouldn't be the first time she had dreamed about her dangerously distracting ex-boss. But the pinch at her toes from Amber's too-small shoes and the noise from the office and reception area were all too real. 'Look, come and get a drink; we can't discuss this in the hall.' And there was safety in numbers.

Safety? Where had that come from? She'd never had even a cross word from the formidable Brazilian before. But then she had never thwarted him before either.

Lightly, lithely for such a tall and muscled man, Deangelo followed her into the office and reception room and the hubbub quietened as he entered. Nobody there would know who he was; he shunned all publicity. Not for his gushing newspaper profiles or charity galas—he protected his privacy with the fierceness of a secret agent—but his sure, confident presence was enough to cast a spell over the moneyed gathering. Avoiding her friends' curious gazes, Harriet led him to a chair in a quiet alcove at the very back of the room. 'I'll get you a drink.'

She didn't need to ask what. It was past six at night which meant no more of the dark, bitter coffee he favoured; instead he'd settle for ice-cold water. No alcohol, not unless entertaining and even then he rarely drank more than one glass. She knew his habits better than she knew her own. She walked quickly into the kitchen and pulled a bottle of sparkling water from the fridge, pouring it into a glass and adding ice and lemon.

Any hope that Deangelo would be on the back foot in Harriet's own space disappeared as soon as she walked back into the office. He sat at perfect ease, his penetrating gaze raking sharply over every object, person and detail in the room, assessing and adding and coming to goodness knew what conclusion. Harriet had never been able to read him. She set the water down in front of him and leaned against the desk opposite. 'Welcome to the Happy Ever After Agency.'

Slowly his gaze returned to meet hers. 'This is a nice house. Yours?'

'No, it belongs to Alex—Alexandra Davenport?' She looked down the room until she located Alex. 'There, by the fireplace. She was your head of media.'

His eyebrows drew together. 'You set up a company with another Aion employee?'

'Three, actually.' Harriet's incurable honesty had her babbling answers to questions he hadn't even asked. 'Emilia Clayton, who headed up events, and Amber Blakeley, who was your client concierge manager.'

For a moment Harriet thought she saw incredulity cross his face, but when she checked again his expression was shuttered as usual. 'You didn't earn enough at Aion?'

'It wasn't about money.'

'Everything's about money,' he said flatly.

'We all earned far more at Aion than we will earn here for several years; maybe we'll never make what we made there. But we all wanted to try to own our own destinies.'

He nodded slowly. 'I can respect that, I suppose, even if I think the risk foolish.'

'You set up your own business.'

His expression closed down even further, just like it always did when she inadvertently touched on anything personal. 'But I had nothing to lose. You had security, a good salary, a good pension. What do you have to gain from this freedom?'

'A family. The four of us, we're like a family.' Harriet snapped her mouth shut. Why on earth had she said that?

Luckily he didn't press it any further. Why would he—what did family have to do with business? 'Tell me, Harriet. What's your price?'

Three years, three long years, she had spent every working hour with this man and not once had he looked at her this way, so intently, as if he could see right into the beating heart of her. She swallowed, fingers itching to grab one of the flutes of champagne Amber was offering round and down it to try and cope with the magnetic focus of Deangelo Santos's full attention.

What was wrong with her? She'd never felt so wrong-footed, so unsure of herself around him before. But then she'd never been quite so aware of him. Never allowed herself to notice how his shirt strained across the broad planes of his shoulders, the barrel of his chest, how physically imposing he was. How magnificent. Her stomach dropped. *Get a grip.* Straightening, Harriet sat up as tall as she could, trying to exude authority and wishing she wasn't perched on a desk. This was her business, her office, her home, after all. She was in charge here.

'I can't help you, I'm afraid. There is too much for me to do here. But I could spend some time with Jenny and help train her in how you like things? Or we do have some excellent temps already signed up. Would you like me to find you someone suitable while HR recruits someone permanent?'

She mentally ran through the CVs she had already received. Deangelo needed a certain type of temp. Someone strong enough to cope with long hours, no thanks or gratitude and brusque interactions, but also someone calm enough to deal with abrupt volte-faces, exceedingly high standards and comfortable working with extremely privileged information. Someone prepared to travel. And, most importantly, someone who wouldn't develop a crush on the very rich, very masculine man lounging opposite her. That was why Jenny had seemed the ideal candidate—experienced and newly married. No rustling, she added to her mental list—whatever that might mean. And no jumping. Maybe she could test for both at interview.

Deangelo leaned forward, his penetrating

gaze still fixed firmly on her. 'I want you to come back.'

Heat suffused her cheeks. 'That's very flattering…'

'I have no interest in flattering you.' That was her told. 'It's a fact. I have an extremely important trip coming up and I need everything to run seamlessly. I don't have time to train someone new or worry about details.'

'The trip to Rio?' She couldn't stop curiosity creeping into her voice. Harriet had no idea why Deangelo had turned his attention to buying a chain of hotels an ocean away. He was from Brazil, but had left at the age of eighteen to take up a scholarship to Cambridge and, as far as she knew, hadn't been back in the intervening twelve years. 'The paperwork was sorted before I left, the jet already notified of your timings, all that was left to do was book the hotel and…'

'I need you to accompany me.' He cut her off ruthlessly. 'All I ask is a month of your time. Then you are free to do whatever you would like.'

Harriet managed to bite back a retort that it was very kind of him. If they could start to supply temps to Aion then that would be a huge coup, exactly the kind of contract that would propel them straight into the top league. But could she really take off when she'd just started up her new business—and, more importantly, did she want to take a step back, even for just a month?

'Why me?'

'This assignment is very—' he paused '—unusual.'

The curiosity she was trying to keep at bay flared. 'Unusual?'

'I need someone I can trust. This is not simply a matter of accompanying me as my PA.'

'Then…' But before she could formulate the question her phone rang. Pulling it out to silence the jaunty tune, she caught sight of the name of the caller, her heart stopping as it flashed on the screen: her father's care home. 'I'm sorry; I really need to take this.'

She barely registered the surprise on Deangelo's face—he probably hadn't been asked to wait once in the ten years since he'd set up Aion as an undergraduate—getting to her feet and walking out of the office and into the mercifully empty kitchen. 'Hello? Harriet Fairchild.'

Numbness consumed her as she listened to the home manager explain that there had been another incident, another fall, that her father's physical health was beginning to deteriorate along with the disease destroying his brain. Blinking back tears, Harriet tried to concentrate as the manager calmly took her through the options for stepping up his care. It was so unfair! So wrong that this should happen to her brave, strong, funny dad, who had cared for her after her mother's death, after already raising her half-sisters alone before that. He'd deserved the most relaxing of retirements, the travels he'd never had a chance to go on, the opportunity to play golf and drink fine wine and read all the books he had planned to get around to. Harriet had never cared that he was older than her friends' fathers, that people often mistook him for her grandfather. He was her wonderful, loving father and she'd do anything for him.

But the truth was she had done all she could; now he needed her the most she had no idea how not to fail him. She'd only got enough for six months' fees as it was. The extras the manager was detailing were bound to be way beyond her reach.

'Yes,' she said at last. 'I understand. Of course. If you could send me a forecast of how much extra you think the enhanced care will cost I would be very grateful.' On auto-pilot she thanked the manager for the home's quick response and promised to be there in time for the doctor's visit in the morning. As she finished the call Harriet stood still for a moment, blinking rapidly to stop the threatened tears, trying to get her face back to cool and professional.

But it was hard to turn her hostess persona back on, not to think about how much this new level of care would cost. Hard not to panic when even six months no longer seemed possible. She could try her sisters again, see if this time they would help out with the cost. Beg them if need be.

They were her last hope. And she knew that meant that she had no hope. 'Damn,' she whispered, the tears this time refusing to be kept away, no matter how she swallowed and blinked.

'Why are you crying?'

How had she not heard Deangelo creep up behind her? Harriet half jumped, swiping her eyes swiftly. 'I'm not,' she lied.

Before she had a chance to compose herself properly, Deangelo had taken hold of her elbow and marched her through the galley kitchen and into the room beyond. The kitchen had been purposely made a contrast to their calm public space, the walls of the narrow room a bright, warm pink, polka-dotted crockery in the same colour on the white-painted dresser. It opened out into a bright glass-roofed conservatory, furnished with a red velvet sofa and chairs and a round table set with four dining chairs. It wasn't a huge space for four grown women to cook, eat and relax in but so far it had done very well. Deangelo deposited her on the sofa before sauntering to the fridge, returning with a large glass of white wine.

'Drink this,' he commented as he handed it over.

'That's Alexandra's; she's the only one with any palate between us.' And the only one happy to spend her hard-earned cash on luxuries like expensive wines and luxury make-up brands.

'Why were you crying?' Deangelo asked again, small talk and niceties dismissed now the tears had stopped.

'It's nothing,' she said, desperate to get the conversation back on track, the thought of the commission from the Aion millions slipping away filling her with panic. 'I'm sorry;

this is so unprofessional. Let's go back to the office and begin again. You said this was an unusual assignment?'

'Is it your father?'

Harriet stared. 'My father?'

'He's in a home, no?' The brusque voice was gentle, Deangelo's usually subtle accent stronger, as if the effort cost him.

'I…yes. How did you know?'

'Harriet, you worked less than six feet away from me for a long time; the door is not soundproof.'

Oh. God. She had always thought him oblivious. Did that mean he had heard every tear-filled begging phone call to her sisters, every long conversation with the healthcare professionals? 'I'm sorry. I always made the time up.'

'Harriet, your professionalism was never in doubt.'

'No.' She closed her eyes for a brief moment, rallying herself. 'My dad has dementia,' she said, the hated words sticking on her tongue. 'He needs specialist care and just before I came to work for you I had to make the difficult decision to put him in a home. I sold his flat to fund it, saved all I could, contributed my own money, but that kind of care is just so expensive and I'm almost out of money, which means I'm going to have to find somewhere a lot cheaper. The problem is he's so settled there. It's like he has a new family. He doesn't ever recognise me any more but he knows his care workers,' she finished sadly.

'And yet you left your job? Why not ask me for a pay rise?'

She couldn't help laughing at that. 'There's no way, even if you doubled my salary, that I could afford to keep him there, not even if I slept in the office and lived on noodles. In a way, knowing there is nothing I could do made my decision to leave a little easier.' The only tiny positive in all the darkness.

'I'll make things even easier. Come with me to Rio and I'll pay for your father's care for as long as he needs it. Do we have a deal?'

'I...' Harriet put the wine glass down carefully, aware she was shaking, hope and grief and adrenaline combining. 'Deangelo, that's very generous.'

'Not at all. You need money and I have plenty.'

'This could be thousands of pounds, tens of thousands.'

But he shrugged as if the vast sums were insignificant. Which for him, she supposed, they were. 'So do we have a deal?'

Yes, her heart cried, but she couldn't agree, not just like that, not without knowing more. 'Just how unusual is this job?'

For one tiny moment Deangelo's gaze shifted, and foreboding stole over her as he spoke.

'I need you to pretend to be my wife. Now, do we have a deal or not?'

CHAPTER THREE

ORDER WAS RESTORED, for now at least. Harriet was back in her rightful place, at her desk, her little cactus by her screen.

Life was back to normal.

Almost…

Deangelo glanced through the open office door to the foyer where Harriet hummed as she typed. On the surface she was her usual efficient self, but something was different and Deangelo couldn't quite put his finger on what it was. Aside from the humming.

She had a sweet, tuneful voice. He'd never realised that before. But then again, she had never sung in front of him before. Maybe that was what was different. Harriet was perfectly respectful, but she was acting more like his equal, business owner to business owner rather than his diffident PA.

The new confidence suited her, added a

glow to her usually pale cheeks and a spring to her step. A step now headed towards him, tablet in hand.

'I just want to check the final timings with you before I head home to pack.' Harriet glanced down at the itinerary she had been adjusting for the last two weeks. 'I can't believe we fly tomorrow. I've never been to South America. Are you looking forward to going home?'

Deangelo frowned. 'Home? London is my home.' He'd created his home, carved it out of grit and stubbornness and flashes of brilliance—or desperation.

'Yes, now, but you grew up in Rio, didn't you?' Her blue, long-lash-fringed eyes were alight with curiosity. 'You must have family and friends there, people you want to catch up with.'

Deangelo had no idea how to answer. His past was a closed book and that was exactly how he wanted it to be. He didn't court publicity, invite questions or disclose any personal details to anyone and there were very good reasons for that. He wasn't ashamed of his rags-to-riches story, or of his climb out of the Rio *favela* to a penthouse on the South Bank. No, it was the other side of his life story he was ashamed of. The side he had taken for granted until it had been ripped away from him. The spoilt boy who had lived in luxury, utterly ignorant of the poverty just feet away from his air-conditioned life.

'We're not there for family.'

Only that wasn't true, was it? His return was all about family. The family that had denied him. The family who had turned their back even as he had swallowed his pride and begged.

'I've been reading up on the city and it sounds incredible; I can't wait to explore a little. Surely there will be time for some sightseeing. Revisiting old haunts?' she pressed.

Haunts was the word. Anywhere he visited in the city would be crawling with ghosts and the kind of memories he had locked away years ago. Deangelo stared out of the window, mouth compressed. Going back was a risk, he knew that. He also knew it might finally set him free. If he dared to reach for it. Funny, he usually thrived on taking risks, but this freedom from the past seemed like a step too far.

'I lost touch with my friends long ago,' he said stiffly. 'I will try and make time to see my aunt, my cousins. If possible.' But it was unlikely. He hadn't even told them he was returning. He knew his aunt wouldn't approve of what he planned to do. He couldn't bear to see disappointment in eyes so similar to his mother's.

Besides, Harriet didn't need to know about his aunt or his cousins, or the work they did for him, work he managed away from the office, away from his PA. Nor did she need to know about the low thrum in his veins, the tingling in his nerves, at the thought of Rio. England was the place where he had reinvented himself, London the city he had conquered, but there was a tinge of grey in his life—grey buildings, grey weather and a grey formality. It suited him, but part of him, the impulsive, hopeful part of him, a part he kept well and truly squashed down, would always hanker for the vibrancy of his childhood home, the colours and the smells and the music. The ability to turn any gathering into a party.

Enough. Deangelo pushed the past back into the past, where it belonged. 'So the itinerary is finalised at last?'

A swift wrinkle between her eyes showed that Harriet had noted the abrupt subject change, but she didn't comment, merely placing her tablet on his desk, the timetable displayed on the screen.

'Yes. You wanted to arrive in the late afternoon so we leave Heathrow early tomorrow morning. A car will meet us on the airfield and it's booked to take us straight to the hotel and your first meeting with the Caetanos is scheduled for the following day. I can't believe how much chopping and changing they've done. I wouldn't be surprised if we get another three rearrangements between now and then.' She didn't add anything else but Deangelo knew she was confused by his acquiescence to the Caetanos' ever-changing schedule when normally such capriciousness would make him walk away.

She placed one delicate fingertip on the screen. 'Okay, hotel. I changed the booking as you requested. I guess it makes sense to stay in the hotel you're buying into but, I have to warn you, it's not up to your usual requirements.' She swiped and a picture of a huge white building studded with balconies and overlooking a golden sweep of sand filled the screen. 'Here you are, The Caetano Palace. As you can see, the position is great, although the hotel is apparently a faded version of its former grandeur; the reviews are less than enthusiastic. I've done some digging on the Caetanos—they're like something out of a soap opera, an old Brazilian family, practically aristocracy. Until around twenty years ago one man, Augusto, controlled the whole business: all the hotels, investments, the lot.' She pressed on a link and the screen changed, Deangelo's chest tightening painfully as he looked down at the photo displayed there. A man in late middle age. Upright, silver-haired, a shrewd look in the laughing eyes.

Augusto Caetano had controlled the company until twenty years ago this very week, the date engraved on what remained of Deangelo's heart. He stayed silent, the old toxic mixture of grief and anger bubbling inside. Grief for the life he hadn't appreciated until it was gone. Not the money, but the safety, the family he had taken for granted. And anger that the safety had been nothing but an illusion. That the man on the screen hadn't cared enough, not when it counted.

'As you have arranged, we're meeting his heirs, the current owners. There are two sons and one daughter, Isabela,' Harriet continued. 'Rumour has it that the business was all they managed to inherit; none of them have the old man's brains. They expanded quickly into luxury island resorts. They aren't popular with the locals or environmentalists from what I can tell. There are claims of bribery and extortion, and complaints of poverty wages for the locals who work at the exclusive resorts, along with some pretty worrying environmental infractions. All this has cost an absolute fortune and so they've been allowing investment by outsiders in order to continue with their spending spree and to keep up their lavish lifestyles.' Harriet's forehead crinkled. 'It doesn't sound like a very good investment, not financially or reputationally.'

'Investment? No. Takeover? Yes.'

'Takeover?' Her eyebrows arched with surprise. 'But the contracts only specify two per cent.'

'When have you known me to bother about two per cent of anything? Fly across the world for something so insignificant? No, Harriet, this is no investment. The Caetanos have been careless. Not only did they sell off a share of the business overall, they've each been chipping away at their own bits, selling a little here and a little there independently. The result? None of them know how much in total has been handed over to outsiders.'

'But you do.' It wasn't a question. He answered it anyway.

'Forty-nine per cent. And even if they knew it was so much, they would assume the majority was held by hundreds of investors all over Brazil and South America, that they can carry on as majority owners unchallenged. Their assumptions would be very wrong. That forty-nine per cent is currently owned by Aion subsidiary companies. Oh, the trail is clear enough, if they had ever bothered to look. I have done nothing illegal, nothing shady. But here we are. They are ready and willing to woo me, not knowing that if they convince me to invest this week, I will hold the controlling stake.' Deangelo's chest tightened in anticipation.

'It seems like a lot of effort for a chain of failing hotels. I mean, yes, the buildings are gorgeous old world creations, but I've been on the review sites and they need a lot of updating. And the islands are incredible, but they're riddled with corruption and bad feeling. If you're planning to own your own hotels wouldn't you be better off starting from scratch?'

'It's not about the hotels, Harriet. It's about justice.'

Justice and fulfilling the promise he'd made to his mother.

Without quite meaning to, he reached up and traced the line of his scar as it bisected his cheek, running his finger along the thin line that ran from forehead to chin. He would make them pay, every one of them, and wipe the Caetano name from the city. No price was too high to pay for that. Abruptly, he changed the subject. 'Anything else?'

'Yes, at least…' She paused. 'It's just when you hired me it was because…' She paused again. Harriet wasn't usually chatty, nor had Deangelo ever seen her lost for words.

He tried to hide his amusement at her un-customary colour and the flustered way she was wringing her hands. 'Because I need you to pose as my wife?'

'Yes. That.' Her colour heightened even more. 'At least, as Marcos Santos's wife. That was the name you wanted me to book the room in?'

'It's still me, I'm afraid,' he said drily. 'Marcos is my middle name.'

As was Deangelo. Luciano, his first name, he'd left behind him in Brazil. Only his father's family had ever used that name anyway; to his mother he had always been Deangelo. Her angel.

'Right. I'm still not clear. Why the name change?'

'Think, Harriet. I have managed to stay out of the press, but this way I can be sure the Caetanos have no idea who I am. If they think Aion are interested in their hotels the price will inflate, but Marcos Santos, CEO of a small tech firm, won't raise any suspicion.' Deangelo clenched his hands into fists. In a way he would have preferred suspicion. Preferred them to remember his middle names. To see him and instantly know who he was. But they had always ignored him. Thought him beneath them. Denied his very existence and claim to kinship. Why, sixteen years after their last encounter, would they suddenly remember his mother's surname, his own full name? Recognise the skinny boy in the man he had become?

Well, the Caetanos would remember. Remember and rue the day they had disowned him and disinherited his mother. He'd make damn sure of that.

Harriet still looked unconvinced. 'The tech firm is one of your subsidiaries, I suppose? Okay, I concede the name change, but I don't understand why you need a wife.'

'To make the meeting seem more like a social gathering, to put them off guard.'

'Right.' She picked up her tablet, her hair falling across her face, a rose gold cloud. 'I hope you don't mind me saying that this whole plan seems utterly insane.'

'You can say whatever you like, as long as you perform your part properly. Just remember we're on our honeymoon and everything will be fine.'

Harriet was already at the door, but as he spoke she stopped and pivoted, eyebrows arched. 'I'm sorry. For a moment I thought you said *honeymoon*.'

'I did. It's the perfect cover. As far as the Caetanos are concerned we are in Rio for our honeymoon and the investment talks are just a side project. I'm ensuring they won't be tempted to look further. I've covered my tracks well, but I'm more comfortable with an extra layer of safeguarding.' Deangelo wasn't sure what the incredulous look on Harriet's face meant, but it didn't seem wholly positive. 'You already agreed to pose as my wife,' he added. 'I'm not asking you to do anything we haven't discussed.'

'*Honeymoon?*'

Surely he'd been quite clear. 'Yes.'

'But—' she gestured wildly, the most exasperated gesture he had ever seen from the usually cool and contained Harriet '—a honeymooning couple is quite, *quite* different to a married couple, you must see that. If we'd been married for ten years or even two, then some kind of coolness, or lack of physical affection wouldn't be noticed. But people expect honeymooners to be, you know, *honeymoony*.'

'Honeymoony?' Was that even a word?

'Yes!'

Deangelo stared at his PA, who seemed uncharacteristically agitated. Her cheeks were flushed a delicate tinge of pink, her lips full and red, her blue eyes brighter. Indignation and embarrassment had stripped her of her professional air and it was as if a veil had been lifted, the full force of her personality shining through, turning conventional prettiness into something deeper and more vibrant.

Something—someone—infinitely more dangerous.

Harriet swallowed and, fascinated, he watched her throat move. When she spoke her voice croaked. 'Does it have to be a honeymoon? It's so intimate. Exposing.'

Intimate. Exposing. Was it getting hot in the office? Deangelo pulled at his collar. 'We're not going to be spending the whole two weeks in Rio with the Caetanos, just the initial meeting when they try and convince me that they're not conning me to invest in a failing business, and the shareholders' meeting a fortnight after. The honeymoon is just a cover, not a role-play. I am recently wealthy, from the wrong side of the tracks, desperate to ally myself with the right people and with my eye firmly off the ball thanks to my new bride. It's not complicated.'

'Even so…' She paused again, biting her lip. 'A honeymoon is really tricky to pull off. If we act just like we usually do then no one will believe that we're newlyweds for more than a minute. You need to convince anyone looking at us that you're mad about me and I need to do the same. Just where people can see us,' she added hurriedly. 'Obviously.'

Deangelo had never been mad about anyone in his life. Never even been tempted to allow a relationship to progress beyond mild desire and liking. But he'd insisted on having Harriet with him for exactly this kind of feedback: not just because he trusted her, but because he also respected her opinion.

'Obviously,' he echoed. 'And how do you propose we convince people we're mad about each other?' The words felt strange on his tongue, heavy and sensuous, and as he spoke them he had a sudden vision of Harriet smiling at him, her hand in his, her lush body warm against him, and with that vision a sense that he was stepping over a line and into the unknown. That the walls around him suddenly didn't feel quite as solid as they always had. He breathed in deep and slow, willing the walls to solidify.

'Well…' She walked back into the office, placing her tablet onto his desk. Deangelo stilled, very aware of her wild strawberry scent, of the curve of her hips, the grace in her long limbs. 'I've not actually been on a honeymoon, but I suppose it's about showing that you're together, standing a little closer than normal, touching each other's hands or arms.' He watched her hand as it fluttered close to his shoulder before jerking firmly away, but he could feel a warm sensation on the tip of his shoulder blade, as if her fingertips rested there.

He straightened, trying to dislodge the

ghostly caress. 'Is that how you behave when you're in love?' He both did and didn't want to know the answer to that question.

'I… I've never actually been in love. I've dated,' she added, chin tilted and eyes bright. 'Obviously. But this isn't about me; it's about what other people do and what they'll expect. Like always looking into each other's eyes. Pet names…'

'Pet names?'

'Yes, you know, like darling or honey or something…'

'In Brazil,' he said, 'we would say *querida, minha amada, me amor.*'

Where had that come from? He never spoke Portuguese any more. Thanks to the private international school he'd attended for his first ten years he'd grown up bilingual, unusual in Brazil, and as soon as he had moved to the UK he'd worked hard to speak, think and even dream in the language of his adopted country. When he could control his dreams that was.

So why was it so easy to imagine saying such words to Harriet?

'Yes,' she said a little unsteadily, stepping back. 'That's the kind of thing. So you see why it would be easier to forget about the whole honeymoon thing.'

'I disagree, *querida*.' Again the endearment slipped out with ease. 'I'm sure we can manage, if we try.'

'Plus—' another step back '—we haven't factored in a honeymoon wardrobe. I own nothing that says bride or rich husband—and I would be surprised if you have a single item suitable for a beach holiday. We're much better sticking to what I assumed was the original script, a wife accompanying her husband on a business trip and dressing accordingly.'

'What do you need?'

'Need?'

'For a honeymoon?'

'Dresses and swimsuits and nice shoes. I don't know, clothes that make me feel special. Sexy.' She bit her lip on the last word as if wanting to recall it, but it hung in the air, thickening it, until Deangelo could hardly breathe.

'Okay then. Take the rest of the afternoon and buy whatever you need. You still have your company card?' Harriet nodded mutely. 'I'll meet you once I've finished here. We can put in some practice at being newlyweds.

Book us in somewhere appropriate. That will be all.'

He didn't allow himself to look up until Harriet had finally left the room, but he could feel her wide blue eyes fixed disbelievingly on him, her scent lingering along with the echoes of that word. *Sexy.* Harriet was bright, incisive, tactful. She was tall and curvy and too demure. She hid her attractiveness behind shapeless clothes and her glorious hair spent most of its life tied up in a tight bun but Deangelo had always seen—seen and resolutely ignored—her potential for real beauty. He had never considered her sexy, though, but now the thought was in his head there was no recalling it. And tonight they would be getting to know each other as newlyweds should.

Only this was all business, and the blood rushing around his body, the thrum of his pulse beating through every pressure point, needed to remember that. Attraction was one thing, acting on it quite another. Not that he had any intention of acting on anything. Fake honeymoon or no fake honeymoon.

CHAPTER FOUR

'THIS WASN'T WHAT I was expecting.' Deangelo turned to the large mirror and grimaced. 'I look ridiculous.'

Harriet suppressed a grin. 'Come on, you weren't born in a suit. You must have worn shorts when you were growing up.'

'Nothing this lurid.'

The shorts were bright, streaks of pinks and oranges and yellows edged with navy. They looked surprisingly good. Deangelo was in fine shape but he wasn't lean; his muscles gave him breadth, his strength apparent in every move. With an effort Harriet pulled her gaze away from the toned brown legs. Thank goodness he was wearing a T-shirt. She couldn't have coped with a bare torso. Which just went to show how crazy this whole honeymoon idea was. Hopefully Deangelo would come to his senses and realise that.

'Pierre is the most sought after personal shopper in London. Amber had to pull in every favour she had to get this appointment as I didn't think you'd want me to use your name. If he says this is what's hot in Brazil right now then you need to trust him.'

The look he gave her from underneath lowered brows promised retribution. 'When I said we would meet to practice being comfortable with each other, I did not mean shopping.'

Harriet was well aware of that. Completely aware that he had expected her to book some exclusive restaurant so that they could sit in an uncomfortable silence and poke at their food. The thought made her stomach twist in panic. Far better to be busy while they sorted out the parameters of what to say and how to be. 'I realised when I was sorting out my clothes for the trip earlier that you could do with a refresh as well.'

'I have clothes.'

She folded her arms. 'Deangelo. You travel, a lot. You must notice that people on holiday do not wear wool suits.'

He shrugged. 'I don't take holidays.'

'No. You don't. But you are claiming to. That means you should be wearing shorts and loose shirts or T-shirts, maybe a couple of light suits but not that…' She waved her hand at his perfectly tailored suit hanging in the dressing room behind him. 'I am completely kitted out now; you need to match.'

Harriet's initial plan to buy just a couple of dresses had been dismissed by Amber, who had accompanied her into Sloane Square and the high-end shops along the King's Road. 'You need to feel the part completely,' her friend had said and, although Harriet had stopped short of the whole new wardrobe Amber had urged on her, she had bought enough clothes for the entire two weeks with cosmetics, accessories and shoes to match, and designer luggage to pack it all in. It was all waiting for her back at the townhouse; tonight she was defiantly wearing one of her own long skirts and baggy blouses, despite Amber trying to persuade her to slip on one of the pretty new dresses for the evening.

She felt safer in her own clothes. More confident, which, after those peculiar moments in Deangelo's office when she hadn't been able to catch her breath, when her chest had seemed to tighten till she could barely speak, her stomach dissolved and her cheeks caught fire, was important. If the mere discussion of pet names and physical closeness could dis-combobulate her in such a way, what would actually acting as a lover be like? Tonight was supposed to be a practice for the next two weeks and she had agreed to that, but it would be on her own terms. And she would be her own person. Straight, boring Harriet in her boring clothes. It was safer that way.

Hopefully the shopping trip that preceded the practice would be the cure she needed, the magic tonic to restore her to her normal professional self. Surely nobody could be at-tractive in lurid board shorts and a matching pink tee, no matter how he was built? She al-lowed herself another peek at Deangelo and stifled a sigh. He had to be the exception that proved the rule. Maybe it was the way the board shorts clung to strong thighs, the T-shirt moulded itself to impressive chest and stomach muscles.

'Stop complaining. This whole escapade was your idea; I'm just trying to make it work.' There, no nonsense and slightly bossy. The perfect PA tone. Boundaries firmly set.

She pretended not to see the gleam in his amber eyes. 'Harriet, you could have ordered me these clothes online. Are you just trying to put the reason for this evening off?'

'Not at all,' she said as airily as she could manage. 'I'm completely prepared for Project Rio.' Giving the next fortnight a codename made it all seem a little easier.

'Project Rio?' But anything else he was planning to say was curtailed by the arrival of Pierre, wheeling a rail which held several pairs of light trousers and a dazzling array of brightly coloured shirts. Harriet sat on the plush sofa designated for waiting friends and family while Deangelo was ushered back into the thickly carpeted and mirrored dressing room. A reprieve. She'd better make the most of it.

Pierre had wheeled all the clothes into the privacy of the dressing room and Harriet suspected she had a lengthy wait in front of her. Taking a sip of the champagne she'd been presented with, and popping one of the delicious dark chocolate truffles into her mouth, she reopened the book she'd started earlier during the suit fittings. But for once the words didn't grab her, absorb her. Instead, every time the hero spoke she saw Deangelo, heard the way his voice had turned to molten honey as he called her *querida*.

Harriet sat back, the book half-closed in her hands. Alexandra was right when she teased her for living through books instead of in the real world. Why wouldn't she? In the books she read families were reunited and dreams came true and love conquered all. Sisters didn't stay away and leave all the burden on one small pair of shoulders, lovers didn't fade away, put off by too many cancelled dates and the reality of dating someone with caring responsibilities. She needed, craved the happy-ever-after she got from books, from her imagination. It was much safer than risking her happiness with someone else. Other people left, even when they didn't mean to. And not always physically or intentionally. Sometimes they just drifted away.

But what wasn't safe was casting her boss, no matter how inadvertently, in the role of hero. Deangelo's longest relationship she knew of had lasted three months—and he had been in Australia for half of that time. His proximity might make her body heat up, but she had to stay cool. She'd been doing so for three years; what difference would another two weeks make?

Suddenly restless, she jumped to her feet and walked to the door of the personal shopping suite, opening it to peer outside. The exclusive department store stayed open late to cater to its demanding customers, and to the tourists who came in to buy small gifts and marvel at the baroque elegance and the designer goods and prices. Her gaze fell on a couple, a few years older than her, flicking through jumpers. The woman pulled one out to hold against the man, desire clear on her face as she surveyed him, before leaning in for a long, lingering kiss. Harriet leaned against the door. Had she ever looked at anyone that way? Had anyone ever looked at her? Had she ever kissed anyone like that, been kissed like that, as if there was nobody else in the world?

The answer was a resounding negative. Nobody had ever treated her as if she was everything. She was safe and reliable—she'd had to be; her father's health had demanded it. But she wanted more. She just needed to be brave enough to step away from her books and find it. Maybe she could practice a little in Brazil, while she was busy being someone else. The kind of woman who owned bikinis and little dresses and whose new husband was mad about her. A taste of the world she was nearly ready to step into.

* * *

Harriet was uncharacteristically quiet as they exited the shop, the clothes Deangelo had picked left behind to be delivered straight to his apartment. His car was waiting for them outside and he directed it to take them back into Chelsea.

'You were right,' he said as the chauffeur pulled out into the lighter than usual evening traffic.

Harriet looked up, surprise widening her eyes. 'I was? Can I have that in writing?'

She smiled, but it seemed forced, not her usual grin, the smile that seemed to come from nowhere to light up her whole face. For the first time Deangelo couldn't help wondering if he had done the right thing. The idea of pretending he was on honeymoon had occurred several weeks ago. He knew his tracks were pretty well covered business-wise, and was as sure as he could be that the Caetanos wouldn't remember that Marcos was his middle name—if they ever spared him a single thought. He doubted it; they'd never come looking for him, after all. But the scar was a problem. Bruno Caetano hadn't stayed around to see what damage he'd inflicted after lashing out at the just fourteen-

year-old Deangelo, but the scar was the first
thing anyone noticed about him, one of the
reasons he preferred to stay in the shadows.
He didn't want them to be sidetracked by it
and start wondering…

Plus there was the family resemblance.
Deangelo had enough of his mother in him
to dilute the fierce hawklike Caetano genes,
but he couldn't rely on the famously self-
absorbed Caetanos not to notice his eyes,
the shape of his jaw. He needed a decoy, a
distraction—and another person seemed the
best way. Someone who would automatically
draw their attention. Who better than a bride,
especially as the Caetanos wouldn't want the
conversation to be too businesslike or for
him to start asking any awkward questions
that might reveal just how tangled their af-
fairs really were?

But asking someone to step into the role
of pretend wife meant allowing them un-
precedented access to his life, to his past.
Even if he concealed his relationship to the
Caetanos, his real reason for the takeover,
and stayed away from his mother's family
and the projects they ran for him, he would
still be returning to Rio de Janeiro for the
first time in twelve years and that made him

vulnerable. Plus, he wanted the whole affair to be as discreet as possible, his role in the Caetanos' downfall hidden. And the only person he trusted absolutely was Harriet.

But he was asking a lot of her. She had her own burdens, burdens he'd watched her carry uncomplainingly, with grace and courage. And one of the reasons she was perfect for the role was that she was as perennially alone as him. There was no jealous boyfriend to protest the charade. But that loneliness made her vulnerable. He had to be aware of that. Work hard to keep the professional distance between them, even as they pretended intimacy.

Good. Now to put his new resolve into action. Deangelo deliberately lightened his tone to something as near to playful as he could manage. 'You're right as in I did need new clothes. The kind of clothes Marco Santos might wear.' The kind of clothes he might have worn if he'd stayed in Brazil and made his fortune there.

'See, you should always listen to me; life is much simpler when you do.'

'It would be easier if you hadn't resigned.'

'True, but you could retain me as a consultant. A couple of hours of advice every week.'

'I might just do that.' Although he kept the light tone the idea appealed to him. Deangelo knew all too well that all relationships were transient, personal and business, but he wasn't ready yet to lose Harriet's quiet common sense. If she wasn't around to be his PA any longer then maybe some kind of consultant role would work.

'At an appropriate hourly rate of course.'

'Naturally. Now, unless you think I need a haircut or new socks or anything else, maybe we could get to the purpose of this evening.'

'Right, Project Rio.'

'Project Rio,' he confirmed. 'Pretending to be newlyweds.'

'Yes. So…er…how do you want to do this?' Her voice trailed off without specifying what *this* actually was.

'It might help if we find out a little more about each other,' Deangelo suggested.

'Or about our personas?' She turned to face him, eyes lit with enthusiasm. 'I mean, I'm not pretending to be married to Deangelo Santos, famously private Brazilian billionaire, CEO of Aion and workaholic, but Marcos Santos. Who is he? And who is he marrying? Not a boring woman of twenty-six whose idea of a fun weekend night is a new book and a clean pair of pyjamas.'

Harriet's words conjured up an irresistible vision of her in simple white pyjamas, curled up on a sofa in front of the fire, book in hand. It wasn't the sexiest vision he'd ever had, but Deangelo's whole body ached with a wish that his life could be so simple and perfect, that his evenings could be spent with something, someone, so uncomplicated and pure.

And that ache, that need, was dangerous. He'd trained himself not to need or want anything other than safety and security. Maybe her idea of being someone else entirely, not just in name, was a good one. A safe option.

'Okay, personas it is. Who is Harriet Santos?'

She sat back, eyes half-closed as she thought. 'How did we meet? Where did we get married?'

Deangelo already knew the answers to her questions, dropped into emails to the Caetanos when setting up the investment. 'We married at the weekend, in New York. We live there.'

Harriet's eyes flew open. 'But I don't know New York!'

'You've been there many times.'

'Yes! But I don't know it; how could I? We get a limousine straight from the steps of your private jet to the hotel. We always stay in some exclusive luxury hotel right in the financial district. We might get another limousine to a Michelin starred restaurant but otherwise you hold all meetings in the hotel. I could be anywhere. I've never actually walked around New York. There's no way I can act like I live there. What's wrong with London?'

'London is too close to the truth.'

She stilled in a way he knew all too well, a way that meant she was thinking furiously, her brain coming up with solution after solution. Her ability to think on her feet was one of the reasons he had employed her, despite her youth, barely in her twenties when she'd started at Aion. 'Okay. I work for a business contact of yours. We met when I was on a business trip with him in New York and you pursued me back to London. We've carried on a long-distance courtship, weekends in Paris and Rome and exclusive resorts where we barely set foot out of the bedroom.' Her cheeks reddened. 'Not that they need to know that explicitly, but we can infer it if they ask too many questions. I haven't had a chance to see New York yet; it's all been so whirlwind. We had a private ceremony at City Hall, but plan to have parties back in New York and London after our month-long honeymoon.'

'Good, that will work.'

'Great. What about you, *Marcos*? Why this investment?'

'Because I want to impress you. I'm not secure in my wealth. I grew up in São Paolo, lower middle class. We got by, but now I have money I want to buy my way into the upper circles of my country, show my bride that I am someone.'

'And how much money does my new husband have?'

'A few million. He founded a tech firm which he's sold on so he's sitting on the profits. The newlyweds are very comfortable indeed.'

'But not in your league?'

'No. And although Marcos Santos probably is richer in real terms than the Caetanos it's not enough to wipe away his nouveau riche stain. Expect the Caetanos to be very condescending.'

'I can cope with condescending.' Harriet's

mouth folded in a way that suggested she had first-hand experience.

'Good. Because we are easy to please and slow to take offence. Overwhelmed with our good luck.'

She nodded and as she did so the car drew up and the chauffeur got out to open her door. 'This isn't my house,' Harriet said in surprise as she exited the car and looked around.

'No.' He followed her out of the car. They were in a pretty tree-lined street, the mighty River Thames just visible in the distance. 'We are about fifteen minutes' walk from your home. I will accompany you there. Maybe we could have a drink on the way. I'll see you back here in an hour,' he told his chauffeur. It wasn't often he walked. Ran, yes. But that was exercise, done for health and to ready his brain for the day ahead. Just to walk, for the sake of the air and the view, with no discernible purpose? He couldn't remember the last time he had done that.

Nor could Harriet, judging by the puzzled look on her face as he turned towards the river. It was a clear spring night, a chill still hanging in the air, stars bright in the purple sky. 'Only two months until the summer equinox,' she said. 'I love this time of year, every day a little more light, a promise of warmth.'

'April showers, wind…'

'It just means we appreciate summer more.'

'I may have lived here for over a third of my life, but I still can't consider what you call summer to *be* summer. A few weeks of humidity and everything coming to a standstill because there's no air conditioning isn't a real summer.'

'That's the true joy of a British summer. You have to plan for rain and cold, hope you get humidity and warmth, but occasionally the skies clear and everything is perfect. Like life, I suppose.' They reached the end of the road, the river path before them, and Deangelo turned left towards Harriet's road, she in step beside him. 'So, it's not that I don't appreciate this starlit walk,' she added. 'But it would have been a lot quicker to just drop me off.'

'But Project Rio isn't finished yet.' Business, just business, he told himself as his heart began to thump. He stopped and held out his hand in silent invitation. Harriet's eyes flew to his. He expected to see uncertainty, distaste, maybe even fear, but instead curiosity gleamed in their blue depths.

'Is this the physical proximity and pet names part of the pretence?'

'That's the one. *Querida*.' He added the endearment as an afterthought, the word thick on his tongue.

'*Querida* sounds so much more romantic than darling or honey.' She made no move to take his hand. 'Which do you prefer?'

Deangelo shrugged. 'Whichever is easiest?'

Twisting her hands together, she looked up at the sky. 'I loved acting at school, wanted to take it further at one point but my dad, well, you know. Anyway, when I was sixteen I was in a play and I had to kiss this boy. I didn't fancy him at all, and he certainly didn't fancy me, that was very clear. It made me realise just what acting meant, the physicality of it. Being put in situations you might not choose. How exposing the business was.'

Of course she didn't want to touch him, not even in pretence. He was monstrous, inside and out. He curled his other hand into a fist, the urge to touch his scar, that physical reminder of his mental wounds, strong.

'But on the night itself it was fine. Somehow we managed this amazing chemistry on stage, despite never interacting off it. And then I realised that acting made you take risks, go places, inhabit feelings you would maybe shy away from. It's a long time since I've done that.' And with that she slipped her hand into his.

Her hand was smooth and cool and fitted into his as if it were meant to be there. Deangelo inhaled. This was acting; she was right. A chance to be someone else for a moment out of time. He started walking again and she fell into step beside him, their conjoined hands between them, an anchor and a barrier. Deangelo was preternaturally aware of her every movement, the swing of her step, the way her hair moved, the swish of her skirt around her ankles. Harriet always dressed like she wanted to fade into the furniture, but the shapeless beige and grey she favoured just set off her hair, her porcelain skin, moving with her body, not concealing it.

Deangelo's pulse sped, beating faster and faster. He wasn't supposed to be thinking of her body, but it was impossible not to when she was near enough to feel her warmth, smell her fresh strawberry scent. What had he been thinking about? Harriet was right.

A honeymooning couple was a ridiculous idea—how could they pull it off for even five seconds? How could he remember who he was and what he needed to do with her so close, the boundaries they so carefully maintained blurred?

'This is my street. You don't need to see me to my door.'

'Fine.' He hadn't noticed that they had reached the road. 'So I'll see you at the airport. A car will come for you at six tomorrow morning.'

'Good. Thanks.'

He nodded brusquely and yet he was exquisitely aware that her hand was still in his. That she had turned towards him, her face tilted towards his, and that same glint of curiosity and adventure danced in her eyes.

'I think,' she said in a low voice, her gaze still fixed on his, 'that you're not really a *babe* or a *hun*, or even a *darling*. *Sweetheart* doesn't work; you're more savoury than sweet. I think I'll keep it simple. How does *love* sound?'

How did it sound? Foreign. Alien. Nobody had spoken a single word of love to him since his mother had died. His aunt had been affectionate in a no-nonsense way, various girlfriends had been romantic when they'd felt it necessary, but love? No. And he preferred it that way. Usually.

Somehow he managed to speak. 'That will be fine.'

Understanding warmed her eyes. 'Okay, love. In that case I'll see you in the morning.' And she rose on her tiptoes and kissed him, a quick, sweet caress on his cheek. Deangelo froze as the warmth from the kiss spread through him at lightning speed and he caught her hand as she pulled away, so she turned to face him again.

'Thank you.' He leaned in only to return the brief kiss, to seal their unspoken contract, but instead of her smooth cheek his mouth found hers, warm and sweet and lush. He froze, every sound, every sensation fading except for her hand in his, her mouth under his. He needed to step back now, apologise, call an end to this whole crazy idea, but before he could move Harriet sighed and, leaning in, deepened the kiss, her free hand creeping up to his shoulder, his own resting on the curve of her waist. It was a sweet kiss, tentative, a millimetre space between their bodies apart from those touch points. The urge to deepen it further thrilled through him, the roaring of his blood drowning out all other sounds, wanting, needing to pull her against him, to feel her curves pressed close, to possess and learn her. But with the thought warning bells sounded loud and clear. He needed nobody, wanted nothing. It was safer. Necessary. He stepped back, releasing her, and instantly the evening chill hit him.

'There,' he said, trying not to notice the dazed look on her face, her sweetly swollen lips. 'I think we're prepared. I'll see you to-morrow.'

He turned without another word and walked away, fighting the urge to go back with every step. Revenge. That was what mattered. And nothing and no one was going to get in his way.

CHAPTER FIVE

'CAN I GET you anything else?'

The receptionist smiled brightly and Harriet summoned up all her courage, stepping closer to Deangelo and slipping her hand through his arm. *Think newlyweds*, she told herself as she leaned into him. *This is quite normal.* But the fizz zipping up her spine was far from normal. Nothing about this situation was normal.

Take her floral sundress, for instance. Not only was it bright and yellow—two words that hadn't described her clothes since she had hit her teens—but it was cut daringly low for a day dress, the pattern louder than she was comfortable with, her wedge sandals precipitously high.

At least Deangelo was also in unfamiliar clothes, his usual handmade suit replaced by chinos and a short-sleeved shirt in a bright blue that contrasted nicely with her yellow dress. He looked good casually dressed, more relaxed. Women still looked at him, not because he exuded wealth and power but because of his sheer attractiveness, the scar and muscle adding a dangerous vibe to his good looks.

No. That was not a road she was going down. Not after the humiliation of last night. Could it have been only yesterday when she had lost herself in a kiss that was nothing but a pretence? Shame and embarrassment engulfed her. But as long as Deangelo didn't suspect the kiss had affected her she could keep her chin high and pretend the whole thing had never happened.

At least neither of them had alluded to it today. They were very much business as usual, the flight taken up with business for the first few hours before Harriet had retired to the smaller cabin, ostensibly to nap and read, in reality to lie on the narrow bed and relive every kiss and brief caress over and over until she'd had to have a Stern Word with herself.

'*Senhora...?*' the receptionist prompted her and, pulling herself together as much as was possible under the circumstances, Harriet looked up at Deangelo with her best imitation of a besotted gaze. She just hoped she didn't look ill instead.

'Thank you, but I think we have everything, don't you, my love?' and if there was an infinitesimal pause before the 'love' and if Deangelo tensed up at her touch just as Harriet tensed up touching him, she didn't think it was too bad an attempt at marital affection.

'*Sim, querida. Obrigado,*' he added to the receptionist, giving her the benefit of his most charming smile, one that was usually only unleashed when he was about to pull off a business coup. Which, Harriet supposed, he was.

'And can I make you dinner reservations for tonight? We have a very fine restaurant here or I could recommend somewhere?' The receptionist's smile widened even further, revealing brilliant white teeth in her perfectly made-up face, her glossy mane of dark hair more suited to a catwalk than a reception desk. But then again, Harriet was beginning to realise that beauty standards in Brazil were very high indeed. Even if she hadn't needed a new wardrobe to play her role as the new Mrs Santos, her sensible work clothes simply wouldn't have cut it here.

Deangelo turned to her, his smile warm and intimate. '*Querida*, what would you like? If you're tired we could always order room service?'

Did he have to make room service sound so very indecent? Harriet wanted to concentrate on the conversation but she was far too aware of the solid feel of Deangelo's arm under her hand, of his hip pressed close to hers, the way she could feel the rise and fall of his breath and how her own breath responded, her heart speeding up at the proximity. If only she didn't know how it felt to hold his hand in hers, how he tasted, decadent and dark and yet tinged with sweetness. Like a sinful dessert, wrong yet so very right.

'Room service sounds perfect. Is that everything? Great, then let's go.'

With an exhaled breath of relief Harriet pulled him away, not caring if the receptionist thought that Harriet was pulling her new husband away from the desk and up to their honeymoon suite with indecent haste.

It took a few minutes for the old lift to reach the top floor where their penthouse suite awaited them. The bellboy escorted them to the ornately gilded door and Harriet waited until Deangelo had tipped him before speaking, doing her best to sound amused rather than hurt. 'I'm not sure you're supposed to flinch when I touch you.'

On the one hand, if Deangelo flinched every time they were in touching distance, then she was in no danger of repeating yesterday's mistake. On the other, no woman wanted to make a man recoil in horror.

'I didn't flinch.'

'Okay. You didn't flinch, you reacted negatively.'

'Harriet, let me make one thing clear.' Harriet's stomach dropped at the low purr in Deangelo's voice and she took an involuntary step backwards, towards the door. 'My reaction was one of surprise, but it was in no way negative.'

'Fine.' Oh, my goodness, was that an actual squeak she'd just emitted? 'I mean, that will make things easier. If we can be positive about this, I mean.' She inhaled, a long deep breath designed to stop her babbling on as much as to try and settle her jangled nerves. 'Okay. I'll set up the office and unpack. Shall I unpack for you, too?' It wasn't one of her normal duties when they were abroad, but then usually they had separate suites.

She would have preferred separate suites this time—with several floors and acres of corridors between them. A safe space where she could hide with her book and her day-dreams.

'I can manage, but thank you.'

'Great!' Another squeak, but at least this one was audible to human ears. 'I'll just check out the rest of the suite.'

It was all going to be fine, she reminded herself. The kind of hotel suites Deangelo stayed in were bigger than most people's flats. Houses in some cases. She would have her own room and bathroom and office and he would be comfortably tucked up in his own bed and everything would be perfectly normal and she just needed to stop thinking about beds before she sent herself crazy...

Grabbing the new designer bag that cost more than her own entire wardrobe, Harriet took a look around the suite. The sitting room was opulent but dated, the heavy velvet curtains and soft furnishings and the bronzes and golds too heavy for the sunny, nature-heavy city she'd passed through, eagerly taking in every sight on the sun-drenched journey from the airport. The furniture was good quality but dark and chipped in places and as she looked around the signs of neglect were clear, from faded paintwork to a missing light bulb. Five-star on the outside, three in reality.

Frowning, she noted that the dining area was situated in an alcove off the sitting room and there was no sign of a separate study. That was going to be awkward; she needed to have some space away from Deangelo. He was so overpowering his presence took over every space. Hopefully there was a desk in her room…

She also didn't see any kind of hallway or corridor, just one door the opposite side to the alcove. She walked slowly to it, dread creeping over her as she turned the ornate glass handle, opening the door to see one huge bedroom. One huge bedroom, with one bathroom, dominated by a bed big enough to sleep an entire family. If, Harriet thought numbly, she was ever called upon to design a nineteenth century bordello, she would be able to draw on the room for inspiration. It featured a lot of red and gold velvet, the bed swathed in heavy curtains.

'Deangelo?' She tried to suppress the

quiver in her voice. 'There's only one bed-room. Only one bed. I'm sorry, I should have made myself clearer when I booked. I'll call down to reception and get them to find us another suite.'

Deangelo stilled. *Dammit.* The last thing he needed was for this trip to slip out of his control in any way. He needed Harriet fo-cused and on game and *he* needed to be fo-cused on the end result as always—and that meant forgetting just how soft Harriet felt when she leaned into him, the way her hip tucked perfectly under his, the light touch of her hand on his forearm. And it certainly meant forgetting about the trusting way she'd accepted his kiss last night, the way she'd re-turned it, stoking it to a heat he hadn't dared contemplate. What would have happened if he hadn't broken it off? He'd not been able to banish the thought all through the sleep-less night.

And that was a big problem. Thoughts and feelings that were nothing but distractions— worse, they were dangerous. Whoever had said that no man was an island was wrong. Every man and woman was exactly that and if they were sensible they stayed that way.

Striding to the door, Deangelo stepped into the oppressively decorated room, his gaze bouncing from gilt mirror to heavy chandelier to oil portrait before finally resting on the huge bed dominating the space. 'How many throw pillows do they think a person needs?' he asked, mentally totting them up and arriving at twelve.

Harriet folded her arms and glared at him, one foot tapping the floor. 'Never mind the pillows, what about the bed?'

He eyed it critically. 'I bet the mattress is soft.'

'Soft or not, there's only one. I didn't think to check. They offered us the best suite in the hotel and that usually means at least two bedrooms. I'm sorry. I'll phone down and see if I could get another room, but I can't order us a new suite or a second bedroom without alerting the kind of questions you need to avoid so either we tell them that you snore so loudly I need a different room or I'll sleep on the sofa.'

'Nonsense. I will sleep on the sofa.'

'No.' Her glare intensified. 'That's ridiculous. I work for you—and this was my mistake. There's no way I am allowing you to sleep anywhere but in that bed.'

'Harriet, I have slept in many places much less comfortable than that sofa, I assure you. Please don't think that I will allow any woman under my protection to not take the bed.' And with that an old memory came unbidden to his mind. He, snug in the one small bed whilst his mother curled up on a pallet on the floor. Shame engulfed him once again and he straightened. 'This conversation is over.'

She glared for one long second. 'Fine. You're the boss.'

'Yes,' he said silkily. 'I am.'

'In that case—' her smile was anything but conciliatory '—I'll leave you in peace. Please close the door behind you.'

To his surprise, Deangelo found himself in retreat for the first time in many years, the bedroom door closed firmly in his face.

He stood there for a second before shrugging and turning away from the firmly closed bedroom door. It was unlike Harriet to show her feelings so clearly, but he preferred annoyance to the dangerous spark that seemed to have ignited between them. Striding over to the curtained windows, he wrenched the heavy drapes aside, cursing the stupidity of people who cloaked such magnificent old windows in overly fancy fabrics. It was one of the many contradictions of Rio that the best views were often to be found in the poorest, most dangerous parts, the *favelas* clinging to the hillsides looking down at the city and sea beyond, but, Deangelo had to admit, this view of Copacabana Beach was gut-wrenchingly beautiful. Miles of golden sand, never-ending blue sea matched by never-ending blue skies. He found the window catch and flung it open, letting the sweet, salty air permeate the room. The air of home.

He was home.

The stone balcony looked as neglected as the rest of the hotel but, after testing it with his foot, Deangelo stepped out, gripping the wrought iron rail as unwanted, long-pushed-away feelings assailed him: nostalgia, grief, anger and a fierce pride at the beauty of his city. A city of contrasts, stunningly beautiful, unbelievably ugly, wealthy beyond belief and horrifically poor. Fun-loving and violent… Rio was all this and more. There was nowhere else like it.

Right now Rio was at its most beguiling. Beneath him, gorgeous people of both sexes sunbathed and paraded perfectly toned bodies shown off by the flimsiest of swimsuits. Children played football on one area of the beach, teens threw a volleyball right next to them, whilst people of all ages swam or waited, surfboard in hand, for the perfect wave, Once he'd been one of those footballing urchins, but never a surfer or a volleyball player and definitely not a beautiful beach boy with no thoughts beyond the sun and the sea. This Rio wasn't his. Could never have been. That was why he had had to leave, to reinvent himself, to lock the part of him that needed and wanted and hoped deep down. He'd thought the chains rusted and the key long lost, but last night, during the brief moments of that kiss, the chains had slackened and for a few beautiful seconds he had needed and wanted and hoped…

'It's beautiful.' Deangelo half turned at the soft voice to see Harriet on the neighbouring balcony gazing wistfully out at the view. 'I've never seen anything like this.'

'You've travelled all over the world.' He didn't mean to sound so brusque, but he also didn't want to get drawn into a talk about Rio, not when his defences were so unexpectedly lowered. He'd thought he'd be able to come here, wrapped in the layers of cynicism and blankness that had kept him safe for all these years, but the combination of revenge so tantalisingly in reach and his new vulnerability around Harriet were battering away at his defences. Made him realise how tired he was of always keeping everyone and anything other than business at arm's length. A curiously hollow feeling ached in his chest. Who knew what would motivate him once he'd achieved his vow, the years stretching ahead devoid of purpose. Making even more money no longer his driving force.

He didn't know how to do anything else, be anyone else.

Harriet stepped closer, her hand still on the stone wall, gaze directed out to the view. She was almost within touching distance; he could reach over the partition that separated them and cover her hand with his. But he wouldn't, no matter how much he wanted to.

'I have been all over the world, you're right. But it's like I said yesterday about New York. I've flown to every continent on your private jet, where we get picked up at the airport by a limousine with blacked-out windows. We're driven to some gorgeous five-star hotel, eat in their world-renowned restaurants and the view from my window is usually the hotel gardens. Sometimes I forget where I am. But this place, despite the Victorian English vibe in there, is real. I'm in Rio. I can't wait to explore. You know—' her voice was wistful and, turning to look at her fully, Deangelo was surprised to see her face was equally so '—everywhere else I went with you I was so busy being the perfect PA I didn't take a single chance to actually see the cities we visited. Sydney or New York, Bangkok or Beijing? Just a hotel room. I'd order room service, use the gym and then read, even when I knew you were busy for hours and wouldn't need me. I think I was just too afraid to venture out alone. But no more. I have to go out and live my life; it's the only one I have and I just can't spend it afraid of what might happen. There's a city out there waiting to be explored and I am going to explore it.'

Wait. *What?*

Deangelo narrowed his eyes, noting the light wrap she'd added to the sundress, the change of shoes from vertiginous sandals to flatter, more comfortable-looking espadrilles, the bag clasped in her hand, her sunglasses. 'You can't go out alone. It's not safe.'

'This is a tourist mecca.'

'Exactly. Where tourists are, so are those who prey on them.'

'Oh, come on. It's early evening, I won't take any expensive jewellery or all my money or anything silly. I'm just going to walk down the street and find somewhere where I can eat and watch the world go by.'

Deangelo could feel the muscle pulsing in his cheek. His plan was simple. Come to the hotel. Get to know his prey up close. Pounce, bite, win. Watch the expression in their eyes as they conceded defeat. Strip all they had from them, including their name, and then return to London—his real home—with his past firmly, once and for all, behind him. What his plan did not include was any kind of engagement with the city which had allowed him to be slung out like trash, the city which had allowed his mother to die for want of affordable treatment.

But he couldn't allow Harriet to go out into Rio's uncertain streets alone. Nor could he forbid her, although that would certainly make things easier. He stood there for a moment, knuckles whitening as he grasped the top of the balcony, contemplating insisting that they had work to do and she would need to do her outing some other time, with a guide he would hire for her. But then he glanced over again and saw the anticipation shining on her face, the excited smile as she stared down at the beach. 'I will come with you,' he said instead, the words almost as much a shock to him as they evidently were to her.

'You don't need to do that.'

'No. But I would like to. If you would allow me?' He made himself add the last part. He had every intention of accompanying her, whether she was comfortable with him there or not.

'It would be nice to have some company,' she said. 'And I suppose it would look a little odd if we went out separately on the first night of our honeymoon. Thank you. I appreciate it.'

'Be ready in five minutes.' Deangelo gave a curt nod before walking back into the hotel room, stomach tightening at the thought of the evening ahead. But whether he was more nervous about going back out into the Rio streets or it was the prospect of spending the evening in an informal setting with a woman he had vowed to maintain a strictly professional relationship with he wasn't sure. Either way, he needed to keep his guard up this evening. The walls he'd erected were there for a reason, to protect him, to protect others from him, and a balmy evening in the *cidade maravilhosa* wouldn't change that, no matter how beautiful and enticing the view—or his companion.

CHAPTER SIX

'I CAN'T BELIEVE I am actually walking on Copacabana Beach.'

Harriet skipped with excitement, her eyes drawn everywhere. For the first few minutes she'd felt self-conscious in her low-cut, floaty dress, her skin so pale that even in the early evening she'd slapped on the factor fifty and a wide-brimmed hat, miserably aware that all those mornings she'd decided on an extra fifteen minutes sleep rather than getting up to run, all those second biscuits and her cake habit meant she would never be able to achieve the toned goddess-like proportions of the women parading up and down in itsy-bitsy bikinis, held up more by luck than gravity. But the sights and sounds were too exciting for her to feel down for long.

Deangelo merely raised a disdainful eyebrow. 'It's looking a little better than the last time I was here, but Copacabana is for tourists. The beach scene is better in Ipanema and some of my favourite beaches are out beyond Leblon. We should be there, or a little north of here, Gávea or Botafogo. Or maybe Santa Teresa.' He slanted an unreadable look her way. 'I think you would like Santa Teresa.'

Was that a good or a bad thing? Harriet made a note to look up Santa Teresa as soon as she got back to the hotel room. 'So why aren't we staying in any of those places?'

'Because the Caetano family offered us a free stay at their flagship Rio hotel and under the circumstances it would have looked odd to refuse.'

'It's a little faded glory.' She watched him carefully as she spoke. Deangelo had made it very clear that they were here to take the hotels over, but he hadn't said why, just stated something obscure about justice. Despite herself, Harriet slid a glance to his scar. She'd been careful when she first went to work with him not to look at it, always keeping her gaze direct and at eye level, and then in time she didn't notice it any more. It wasn't the scar itself that was so shocking, it had healed to a thin, puckered white line; it was more the length of it that jarred. At some point Deangelo's face had been torn apart and no one she knew had any idea why. Was that the justice he spoke of? Were the Caetanos responsible for the scar? For the closed-off way he lived, alone and shut away?

If so, she would happily take everything they owned away from them herself.

Because it was increasingly clear that whatever, whoever had shaped him had scarred him inside and out. But he hadn't been closed off last night. Try as she might, she couldn't forget the moment his hand had slipped around her waist and the kiss had caught fire. He had wanted her, she was almost sure, even in her relative inexperience. There had been something about the careful way he had held her—and released her—that had suggested that he was only just keeping control.

Or was that wishful thinking on her side? Allowing her imagination to run away with what might have meant nothing at all?

Either way, she had made that happen. Hadn't stepped back in shock after his brief caress. No, she had demanded more and for a brief time had got it. It was a lesson to her to be bolder. What was the worst that could happen? She was used to rejection. She shouldn't fear it. She tried to imagine taking hold of his hand, strong and tanned and so close, but her imagination, usually so vibrant, failed her.

Coward, she told herself.

'Back in the nineteen-twenties the Caetano Palace was one of the most prestigious hotels in the city, if not the country,' Deangelo said, and Harriet turned her attention back to the conversation with some relief. 'It's that name, that history they want me to invest in. And,' he added, 'the kind of businessman naïve enough to want to make this kind of investment is the kind who would think staying right here is the epitome of sophistication. Still, once the deal is complete we'll move somewhere more appropriate.'

'Well, I think Copacabana is beautiful. Everyone seems to be having a good time. You know, I still can't get my head around how big Brazil actually is. In my head there's Rio and then the Amazon, but that's like saying Europe is Paris and the Danube and missing out on all the other cities and coasts and rivers. Is there anywhere I should try and visit while I have the opportunity? There's a few free days in the itinerary and if you can spare me I'd like to see something of the country.' This was the start of a new page—she was going to live her life, not just read about other people's.

Deangelo didn't answer for a long moment, as unreadable as ever. She'd worked for him for three years and still knew nothing about him apart from his coffee order. He never took leave so she didn't know the kind of holiday he enjoyed, she'd never seen him read a book, heard him listen to music. When he finally spoke, his voice was so quiet she could barely make out the words. 'I don't know anywhere in Brazil but here; the first time I left Rio I was eighteen and on a plane to England.'

Harriet opened her mouth but could find no words, so shut it again, feeling a little like a landed fish. Deangelo was so sure of himself, he was the very epitome of sophistication. She knew nothing about his past, but she'd assumed he came from money, or at least a comfortable existence. Everything about him exuded privilege, from the way he wore his handmade suits to his austere but impeccable taste. He'd been educated at Cambridge, for goodness' sake.

But he'd never mentioned his family, or even a single childhood anecdote. Maybe the slight hint of street fighter, one amplified by the scar on his cheek, was more than a hint. Harriet glanced around again, her gaze alighting on a gaggle of boys kicking a football, their clothes old and worn, feet bare, hair cropped close to their heads. She looked back at Deangelo and saw his gaze also fixed on the boys, a bleak sadness in his eyes, and realised with a jolt he saw himself in their skinny limbs and dirty clothes.

'Come on,' she said, desperate to change the subject and wipe that sadness out of his amber eyes. 'Let's get some food. I'm hungry.'

Harriet swiftly overruled Deangelo's suggestion that they look for one of the new crop of critically acclaimed restaurants that had recently opened up as Copacabana tried to shake off its slightly seedy tag. 'You came along on my evening out, remember?' she said. 'And I don't want fine dining. I want to sit and soak in the atmosphere. In fact—' her eye was caught by one of the kiosks that were prevalent along the golden strip of sand '—let's eat here.'

'At a kiosk? Outside?' He couldn't have

sounded more outraged if she'd suggested stealing food out of the hands of the small group of children picnicking nearby.

'Sounds perfect, doesn't it? Let's see what they're serving.'

They had passed several of the iconic beach kiosks, some the traditional wood, others, like the one they were approaching, a silver metal glinting in the sun. The large round kiosk was surrounded by several tables, each shielded from the sun by a huge umbrella, all with an unparalleled view of the sea. From the kiosk itself an enticing smell wafted out and Harriet realised just how very hungry she was. She peered over at the menu, squinting as she tried to read the scrawling handwritten sign. 'They serve *espettos*—they smell good, whatever they are.'

'Kebabs,' Deangelo told her. 'Usually meat or fish, sometimes vegetables.'

'Perfect. I'll get these; what would you like?'

It took a few minutes to convince Deangelo that she both could and would buy dinner, his argument that she'd only be claiming the dinner back on expenses waved away. 'It doesn't matter that I'll be using the corporate card. I want to go up and order the food.' She knew it sounded a little pointless, but Harriet had spent so long *not* doing, waiting for life to start, she just didn't want to wait any more, just like she hadn't wanted to spend another night waiting for room service in an anonymous hotel room.

The young man in the kiosk was perfectly charming, praising her halting phrasebook Portuguese, his appreciative gaze resting on her in a way that managed to combine respectfulness with a playful flirtatiousness and a sense that if Harriet was willing the flirtatiousness would be amped up. She'd never been flirted with quite so expertly before and carried the cold beers back over to the table where Deangelo sat glowering, feeling sexier and more feminine than she had for a long, long time. 'I ordered a selection so we can try all the different types, along with bread and salad; is that okay? What's wrong?' she asked, as his glower intensified.

'Was that boy being disrespectful?'

'What? Who? No! He was being nice. He's not really interested in me, I'm at least a decade older. But I appreciated the gesture, he flirted so charmingly.'

'As far as he is aware you're a married woman.' The glower intensified and a sense of the absurd mingled with a weird moment of wishing this was real, that she really was carrying the drinks back to someone who cared deeply about her, deeply enough to mistake practised flirtation for genuine interest. Harriet inhaled, trying to quell that note of wistfulness. Deangelo was being overprotective, that was all.

'Actually, there's one thing we forgot.' She held up her bare left hand. 'No ring, so he couldn't have known about any marriage, real or fake. But I was thinking we'd say we left the rings behind because of safety concerns, so there's no need for us to buy any.' Harriet wasn't comfortable about accepting valuable jewellery, even temporarily, and the thought of wearing rings on her fourth finger made her uncomfortable in ways she didn't know how to articulate.

Deangelo's frown merely deepened. 'It's been taken care of; they will be here tomorrow.'

Wait, what? 'No, no, there's no need. Honestly.'

His brows drew together but, before he could respond, the waiter brought over a bowl filled with delicious-smelling bread, a mixture between a dough ball and a bread roll, and the conversation stalled as the delicious aroma floated towards them. Harriet managed to remember her manners and wait until the bowl had been set down before picking up a roll, her stomach gurgling in anticipation. The roll was still warm as she bit into it, the texture crisp on the outside, soft in the middle and filled with cheese. 'Oh, my goodness. These are amazing.'

She looked over at Deangelo for confirmation and, to her surprise, his face had softened to a melancholy nostalgia. '*Pão de queijo.* My mother used to make them. I haven't had these since I left Brazil.'

'There must be somewhere in London you could buy them. Now I've discovered them I'm not going to let them simply walk out of my life. This is a long-term relationship, I can just tell.'

But Deangelo was shaking his head. 'In London I like to forget about Brazil. There's no time to look back. Living in the past is for fools. Better to move on, find new things.'

'But—' Harriet said, watching him carefully as she spoke; this could be her chance to find out exactly what was going on '—you're back here, playing games to buy an overpriced money pit hotel chain. It can't be a coincidence that you've chosen to do something so uncharacteristic in the city you grew up in...'

His expression shut down immediately. Harriet had never realised before just how high the walls were that Deangelo lived behind. Nor just how much he cut himself off from all human interaction. She knew his existence was focused, that he didn't socialise or relax, that he had no hobbies and he had no obvious vices nor any obvious virtues. He ignored the many fundraising messages that crossed her desk—no gala balls for him, no charity concerts. He *chose* to live alone, whereas circumstances had meant that for too many years she had had little interaction with people outside work. The loneliness had nearly broken her. How could he choose to live like this? How could he bear it?

But then again, he had bought her that beautiful cashmere coat last Christmas. It had fitted her like a glove, the colour bringing out the blue of her eyes. It was the most beautiful thing she'd ever owned. For her birthday he'd given her lifetime membership to the London Library, a gift she hadn't realised she'd coveted until she received it. He must have noticed that she always had a book or two in her bag, that her only spending splurges were on books…

He must have noticed her…

She looked across and realised he was watching her intently, warmth suffusing her as his gaze seemed to strip her to the bones, see inside her. She tried to suppress a shiver, the urge to reach out and touch him almost overwhelming her. She wanted to feel his touch again and, God help her, she wanted him to kiss her again.

With the first bite of the herby, cheese-filled bread he was home, seeing his mother balling the dough, slapping away his hands as he had tried to grab the cheese. Grief, for her and the innocent boy he had been, rose thickly in his throat and Deangelo washed the roll down with a swig of beer, almost afraid of the emotions one taste had unleashed, afraid of the urge to confess his sins to the woman opposite him as her gaze snagged his, warmth and understanding in her smile and something that looked very like desire in the depths of her clear blue eyes. His own body responded instantly, blood heating as he allowed himself one long look, one moment of pretending that this was, could be, real before tearing his gaze away. Why would a woman like Harriet, one with so much to give, want a man who was nothing, despite the billions in the bank?

Suddenly he wanted to know the heart of her, even if he could, should, do nothing with that information. 'You told me you left Aion to build a family. What did you mean?'

Harriet picked up another of the cheese balls and began to tear small pieces off it as she looked over towards the sea, her gaze wistful. Deangelo followed her line of sight, his eyes resting on a family playing on the beach, the parents laughing as they threw a ball to their small children, smiles filled with love and pride. 'Like I said, I just wanted a family.' Her voice was so low Deangelo wasn't even sure he'd heard her correctly. He snapped his gaze back to her. The loneliness in her eyes would be like looking in a mirror, if he ever allowed himself to feel anything at all.

'You have a family. Your father...'

'I love my dad more than anything. At least, I love the man he used to be more than anything. I can't help but resent the person he is now.' She ripped another roll to shreds, then pushed her plate away. 'It's like my own dad was kidnapped and replaced with a stranger who looks like him but is in no way my funny, kind daddy. But then occasionally there are glimpses and I know he's trapped in there somewhere. Those moments are the worst of all.' She looked up, stricken. 'I don't mean that exactly...'

'And you have no other family?'

Harriet shook her head. 'Both my parents were only children and already pretty elderly when I was born—it was a second marriage for both of them. Mum said I was her late life miracle. She died when I was eleven, so it was just me and Dad. I do have two half-sisters, but they resented my mother—and me, I think—and I don't see much of them.'

Deangelo couldn't help but see the parallels. One dead parent, one ill parent and a family who weren't interested in helping out. Some stories were universal, and always damaging. 'Don't your sisters help out with your father?'

'No.' There was a world of heartbreak in that answer. Deangelo could have warned her—never put your faith in the goodness of others. But it was clearly too late for Harriet.

'No,' she repeated. 'Like I said, they resented me, resented Mum. They loved the big house Dad provided, their allowances and cars and horses and all the rest of it. Dad was a merchant banker. He worked so hard; Mum was always telling him to slow down. He'd leave for work really early, come back late.' Her face softened. 'On Thursday night he'd always ask us what we wanted him to bring home for the weekend. My mother always asked for flowers and so I did, too; I wanted to be just like her. My sisters laughed at me for that but I loved it when he'd present me with a perfect rose. I'd give anything for him to give me a rose one last time.' She blinked rapidly, before taking a long swig of her beer.

'Anyway, after Mum died he decided he needed to cut his hours, to look after me. He quit his job to become a lecturer at LSE, and sold our house so we could live close to his work. He bought a flat in Crouch End and shared the rest of the money between us; mine was supposed to put me through university. My sisters were appalled; they couldn't bear the loss of their lifestyle but, to be fair, they took that money and multiplied it. They own a chain of tanning and beauty shops; they do really well. But when I asked if they would help out with his costs they didn't even return my calls. They haven't visited him—or me—in years.'

'And your share of the money?'

He was sure of her answer and unsurprised when she answered. 'Oh, well, it was clear Dad was having problems when I was still at school. By the time I was eighteen, leaving him so I could head to university was out of the question so I did a PA course, working part-time so I could look after him. We managed okay for a few years, but then it was more than I could do on my own; he just wasn't safe to leave on his own. I felt so guilty. So guilty.' She stopped, swallowed. 'If I couldn't look after him then he had to have the best and if that meant selling the flat and donating my trust fund to pay for it then of course that's what I would do. Only this meant I needed a full-time job—and to pay rent—so I got a job at Aion. A year later I was promoted to work for you. I thought maybe things would change for me, but they didn't. I'd lost part of myself in those years with Dad. My confidence maybe? Sense of self. Whatever it was, I just seemed to be as lonely as ever.'

She stared out at the beach. 'When you

spend your teens and early twenties looking after your dad it's hard to meet people and relationships are pretty much out of the question. I lost touch with my school friends and going out in the evening was impossible anyway. Once I started renting it didn't get easier. London can be pretty anonymous when you don't have money or connections and you have to keep moving because rents are so expensive. And then I met the girls.'

'The girls?'

'Emilia, Alex and Amber. The Christmas after I had just started working directly for you. It was Christmas Eve and we were all free to go at noon, only I had nowhere to go so I stayed.'

Dimly, Deangelo remembered. He usually worked over Christmas, so hadn't thought it odd that Harriet had stayed until six. 'I didn't know.' And if he had what would he have done? Probably nothing. Other people's tragedies weren't his business.

She smiled a brief sad smile. 'How could you? Anyway. I finally left. I was dreading Christmas Eve evening more than Christmas Day in some ways. I had planned a walk, bought some food for the day itself, but the evening seemed unbearably long. And then in the lift I met Alex. I didn't really know her—she's a little intimidating, so posh and cool, you know? Anyway. I asked her if she had any nice plans for that evening and she just looked, for one second, as bleak as I felt and said no. It was a takeaway and an early night. So I gathered up all my courage and suggested a drink. To my shock, she said yes.'

Her mouth softened. 'We gathered up Emilia in the lobby; she was trying to get up the courage to walk out into the lonely night. Amber was outside, fruitlessly trying to find a taxi. We went out for wine and pizza and it was the best Christmas Eve I had had in about ten years. The next day we met and walked through Hyde Park then found a little café selling fry-ups and had bacon and eggs for our Christmas lunch. And somehow we knew. We had found a family, not one of blood but a family nonetheless. A year later we started talking about setting up an agency and here we are.'

The arrival of the *espettos* interrupted anything Deangelo might have said, but he couldn't help but mark the difference between them. Life had stripped all they loved from them, but he had closed himself off and made money, each million, each billion, another brick in the wall separating him from humanity. From feelings. But Harriet? Rejected by what remained of her family, she'd gone out and built herself another one. He had made money but she was the richer by far.

Harriet deserved all the love, all the happiness in the world. He'd lifted her financial burden from her; the least he could do was to make this final fortnight together special too. Show her the real Rio de Janeiro, even if it meant showing her a tiny part of the real Deangelo Santos, too. Show her just how worthy of love and happiness she was. One final gift. Before she walked out of his life for ever.

CHAPTER SEVEN

WHAT WAS WRONG with her? One beach walk and one kiss and she was spilling her guts like a low-level hoodlum with a plea bargain. Harriet cringed. How could she have said so much? It was so unlike her—and so unprofessional. So exposing.

But for a moment there, the amber eyes had been full of empathy, as if he truly knew what it felt like to have nothing, to have no one.

'These are good,' she said a little awkwardly, picking up an *espetto* and waving it around. 'First night and I'm already converted to Brazilian food. What else do I need to do to fit in around here?'

'Sport.' Deangelo nodded at the footballers to one side and the volleyballers on the other just as, as if to prove his point, a gorgeous couple jogged past. 'Football, of course. It's not just the national passion, it's the national reason for existing.'

'I don't mind football. My dad supported Arsenal.'

'Don't mind is better than nothing. But it lacks passion, and passion is one of the most important Brazilian traits. If you want to know Brazil, then you must remember this…' He leaned forward, eyes molten gold, reflecting the evening sun. 'Brazil is a land of hedonism, of pleasure and relaxation and sensuality.'

Harriet swallowed, almost choking on her bread. 'It's *what*?'

'Oh, we don't mind work.' His usually almost imperceptible accent deepened. 'After all, it takes a lot of dedication to look like that.' He waved his hand towards a group of young people drinking at the counter, the girls in tiny dresses showing off lean, toned limbs and dramatic curves, the men all chiselled as if carved by Michelangelo himself. 'But Brazilians don't sweat the small stuff; we like to make sure there's plenty of time to enjoy the finer things in life. Food, music, the outside, love, dance…'

The way he lingered on *love* called to mind something a lot more carnal than romantic, a physicality inherent in the word, and she was instantly transported back to last night, her hand in his, the feel of his shoulder, strong under her palm, the decadent richness of the kiss. Warmth suffused her cheeks, spreading down to touch every part of her.

This was ridiculous. Her love life might have been sedate since she had first found her father looking for the cat that had died several years ago and realised that the loss of words and forgetfulness was not a natural part of ageing but something infinitely more sinister, but she hadn't been in a convent. There had been other kisses, even a two-year relationship that had died a natural death as her father's needs had intensified and she simply had no more emotional give in her. She needed to pull herself together—and then when she got home allow Amber to sign her up to a dating app. Her friend had been trying to persuade her for long enough.

'Dance?' she said, as coolly as she could, despite the intensity in his face, his scar setting off his saturnine handsomeness rather than marring it, reminding her he was both out of her league and her skillset.

'Of course. In Argentina they like to tango. To follow rules, to embody drama and violence and repression. In Brazil we samba. The samba is all about passion. About being free.' His gaze met hers, bold and intense, and Harriet shivered at the wildness in the depths of his eyes.

Passion? Where had this come from? Deangelo was the kind of man who probably slept in his suit. He was organised and predictable and proper. But her body knew full well he hadn't been any of those things last night and, good intentions aside, how could she be anything but intrigued by the dangerous glint in his eyes, the wolfish smile playing on his sensual mouth?

Swallowing hard, she tried to drag the conversation and her mind back on track. 'Samba? That's the dance with the bright costumes, right? All feathers and big hats?' And barely-there outfits, but she wasn't going to mention that.

'Traditionally yes, but samba is more than costume. A samba can be danced in any clothes at any time. It's about rhythm, about intent. It comes from the heart, through the hips.'

'The hips, right. Then I'd better not give

it a go. My attempts at baby ballet were not a success. Dance is obviously not for me.'

She was doing the right thing, responding sensibly, not allowing the sensual haze creeping up to envelop her. Last night was a one-off—and Deangelo had ended it before it had gone anywhere. She was putting it firmly behind her to concentrate on enjoying this opportunity to explore Brazil. So why did she feel like a coward, a sense of opportunities lost once again creeping over her?

She was tired of doing the sensible thing— after all, even quitting her job to set up the Happy Ever After Agency had been cushioned by Alexandra's inheritance and the knowledge that, no matter what, she would have a roof over her head. She was in a city known for its laid-back attitude, a city made for fun, for letting go. What was it Alexandra had said, the first time they had discussed working for themselves? 'You can't experience life through books alone, Harriet. At some point you have to go out and start living it.'

Harriet had laughed the comment off, clutching her beloved romance hardback to her, exclaiming that all she needed was in the pages of the book. But the words had stayed with her, came back to her now.

Something had changed in the last twenty-four hours. For her, for them. A line had been crossed and there was no going back, not now she'd finally admitted to herself just how attracted she was to Deangelo. Desire flaring in the pit of her stomach, warming her whole body, setting every nerve on edge with awareness. Awareness of his surprisingly elegant hands, the broadness of his shoulders, the muscles that could make him seem heavyset if he didn't move with such lithe grace, the sensual lines of his mouth, his heavy brows, the utter masculinity of a face that wasn't handsome exactly, but undeniably attractive, the scar running down his cheek adding a rakish sensuality. For the first time Harriet knew why rooms went quiet when Deangelo strode in, why every woman, and plenty of the men, turned as if magnetically pulled in his direction. It wasn't just the money or the power; it was utter sensuality. How had she not noticed before?

Or maybe she had noticed but hid it even from herself.

He sat back, eyes issuing a challenge she knew she was going to accept. 'English people can't samba because they have no idea how to let go.'

Harriet narrowed her eyes at the dismissive comment. 'You live in England now.'

'It suits me. I like the control. I'm not criticising the English; I'm just stating a fact. You said yourself, you couldn't even manage ballet, and ballet is all about rules. The samba twists the rules…'

'So, let me get this straight. You like the rules yourself, but can still let go enough to samba?'

'If I chose to, of course.'

'Okay then.' Harriet pushed back her chair, standing up, nerves competing with an excitement she couldn't quite name. 'Prove it.'

He didn't move for one long moment, only a pulse beating in his jaw showing any sign of life at all. Harriet stood still, watching him, the nerves tumbling in her stomach, her whole body aching with the need to act, to do. This evening was already unusual: the sharing of a meal, the location, the frank speech. Why not carry it on, rediscover the easy intimacy they had shared last night, would need for tomorrow? Then they would, no doubt, move on, to another hotel where they had their own space and normality would resume until they returned home and she walked away once again.

Besides, she was intrigued. This was his home. She knew little more about the enigmatic billionaire than anyone else, despite their close proximity. The opportunity to find out who he really was seemed too good an opportunity to pass up.

But, more than anything, she wanted to keep feeling the way she did right now: full of possibilities and possibility. Attracted and attractive. Desiring and desired. Because there had been a minute there, when his gaze had locked on hers, when something had flickered between them, something new and dangerous.

She'd been good for so very long.

She needed to start living outside the pages of her book.

And it was only one dance.

So she waited, her gaze locked on his, daring, provocative until he nodded. One firm gesture.

'So be it.'

There was only one place to samba. Oh, sure, there were bars all over Rio, even a couple of decent ones here in Copacabana, but to really get to the heart of the dance then they needed to head to Lapa. Without a word to Harriet, Deangelo summoned a taxi, ushering Harriet into the back, joining her as the car headed along the beach.

This was crazy; he knew that. Crazy on so many levels he didn't even know where to begin. To spend an evening together like this under normal circumstances was risky; to do so in the city of his birth, in the city where all his secrets lay buried, was playing with fire.

And that was before he considered the change in Harriet this evening. It wasn't just physical, although he wasn't used to seeing her strawberry-blonde hair loose, her lush curves shown off rather than hidden away by sensible if shapeless office wear. It wasn't the bolder way she interacted with him, her usual reserve replaced with a sharp curiosity and a new openness. It was the way she made him feel: a little protective, a little possessive, as if he wanted to show her his world, impress her. As if he wanted her to know him, the real him. And that was the most dangerous thing of all.

But he was in Rio. Tomorrow the game would begin. Tonight was his.

At one time he'd known all the bars in Lapa. The ones where the tourists were funnelled to, the ones they'd never see. The places where only the best dancers took to the floor, and those where every beginner was welcome. Tiny bars carved into alleyways, large glitzy bars where light glittered from every sequin. Would they recognise him if he went there? Unlikely; back then he'd just been another street rat.

No. Not a bar. He wanted to make this visit special for Harriet; that meant taking her to the very best, most spectacular place.

Harriet didn't speak as they travelled through the darkening streets, staring out of the windows, concentrating on every street scene they passed, absorbing the city, but she let out a gasp as the car pulled up outside the grand stone building. It looked impressive, every window ornately decorated with stone carvings, lights blazing from the open double doors at the top of the wide steps. Deangelo helped Harriet from the taxi, keeping her hand in his as they started to ascend the steps, trying not to notice how much her touch felt like home as he led her into the huge hallway, light bouncing off a dozen chandeliers. Deangelo kept hold of her even as he muttered a few words to the hostess greeting them, and they followed her to a corner table, one both discreet and yet with an enviable view of the dance floor.

It was still early but the room was already half-filled and couples had taken to the floor, showcasing moves that would win awards in Europe, music filling the room from the stage at the other end of the room, the musicians already lost to the beat. Usually he would have ordered the ice-cold beer customary in these establishments but, after glancing at Harriet, her eyes shining as she took in the scene, Deangelo changed his mind and ordered champagne.

'This is incredible.' Harriet took her seat, still transfixed by the dancing in front of her. 'When do the normal people start dancing?'

'These are the normal people.'

'What?' She turned and stared at him. 'They can't be! Look at her feet. And his—and that leg-kick. Normal people can't do that.'

'They can in the *gafieiras*. But everyone is welcome, whatever their level.'

A bow-tied waiter interrupted them at that moment, a bottle of champagne in an ice bucket in one hand, two frosted glasses in the other, and conversation stopped as the cork was popped, the champagne poured and Harriet sat back, glass in hand, to watch the dancing.

The beat swelled, the music thumping through him, every note, every key change calling to him. Almost without noticing, his foot began to tap along, his body to shift in time with the beat. The room was steadily filling and the accomplished dancers on the floor were joined by more and more couples, of much more varying levels, including a few tourists who, although clearly game, had more enthusiasm than ability; they were soon swooped upon by experienced dancers who whirled them away to teach them the proper steps to their evident equal delight and trepidation.

It was time.

Deangelo pushed himself to his feet and held out a hand. 'Come along.'

Harriet clutched her glass. 'What do you mean?'

'You wanted to learn how to be a Brazilian? Right there.' He nodded at the dance floor. 'That's where you'll find out.'

She clutched the glass harder. 'I can't go out there!'

'Why not? If he can—' he nodded at a rotund tourist, furiously jiggling away, his face serious as he tried to remember the steps his partner was teaching him '—you definitely can.'

'But…'

He didn't wait for her to finish the sentence, removing the glass from her hand and drawing her to her feet.

'The thing to remember about samba,' he said, 'is you have to find the rhythm. It's three steps to two beats, the middle step is the quick one. Once you have that, then add bounce, keep your knees soft. So it's back, feet together, forward…' They were on the dance floor and Deangelo swept her into his arms, murmuring the steps to her. 'That's it, back, together, forward, knees bent, let your body roll through the steps, don't be afraid to roll your hips.'

Harriet was clearly nervous, clutching his hand as she shuffled through the steps, her eyes on her feet.

'Look at me,' he murmured. 'Feel the beat; let it guide you.'

The music was getting louder and louder, the beat stronger and more insistent, the dance floor busier and busier. Deangelo lost track of time, knowing nothing but the woman in his arms, the softness of her under his hands, the way his pulse was connected to the music, the light in her blue eyes as she moved, the sheen of perspiration on her forehead as the heat intensified. How had he thought running would be the same as dancing? The solitary sport against this communal celebration of music and passion? No wonder he'd only felt half-alive the last twelve years, replacing joy with monotony, the thud of his feet on the pavement instead of the thud of his heart to the beat. It was necessary, that half-life, but such a relief to let the walls tumble for one night, to let the young man who had loved and laughed and dreamed emerge from the cold professional persona he was caged in. Tomorrow would be time enough to tame him again.

As Harriet got more confident he encouraged her to move in a processional step, her hips moving as if she'd been born to do this, hair swirling in time with the beat. He twirled her, then twirled her back and Harriet lost her footing, falling into him, her face upturned, laughing. Time slowed, each musical note drawn out to an almost unbearable crescendo, every couple moving in slow motion. All Deangelo could see was Harriet's parted mouth, her laughing eyes, all he could feel was her soft weight colliding with his, her breasts against his chest, hip to hip, leg to leg, the heat of her, her pulse racing in unison with his.

He was consumed by her and all she represented—freedom and need and happiness and sensuality—hair around her shoulders, her dress slipping off her shoulders, revealing the deep vee of her breasts, her lush mouth tilted towards his as if offering. How could he resist?

He'd been the king of resistance for so many long years, ruthlessly squashing any need and want that didn't align with his goal. Not for him romance or love. Not for him the false comfort of human relationships. Work and enough exercise to keep his body and mind fighting fit. That was enough. That was all he allowed himself. Harriet represented all that was forbidden. That was what made her so intoxicating.

He could still have walked away, led her back to their table, called a taxi and escorted her back to the hotel, put tonight down to courtesy, if she hadn't moved in a little closer, if her hand hadn't slipped around his waist, if she hadn't put her other hand on his shoulder, aligning herself even closer to him. If she hadn't flicked her tongue nervously over her mouth, her eyes fixed on his. She wanted him and he was powerless to resist, the memory of how sweet her kiss felt consuming him.

His hand slid down her back to the glorious curve of her hip, his gaze watching her throughout the slow caress, waiting for further permission. She sighed as her eyelids fluttered shut, leaning in to his touch, her own hands tightening their grip. Permission granted.

The first kiss was fleeting, a mere brush of lips. She tasted of champagne sweetened with honey, her mouth soft under his. The second kiss was barely a second longer, Deangelo still needing to know that this was what she wanted.

Once again it was Harriet who made the next move, standing on her tiptoes to press her mouth to his, opening up under him. This was no mere brush, no polite enquiry. Deangelo pulled her tight against him, deepening the kiss, his hands roaming over her body as they moved to the beat of the drums, stepping in perfect time, hips moving, lost in the rhythm they created.

With an effort, Deangelo pulled himself away. 'Want to get out of here?'

'Can we return? Before we leave Rio?'

'It's a date.' The words were out of his mouth before he could stop them and he paused. 'I mean…'

But she laid a finger over his mouth. 'No. You don't have to say anything. I know what this is.'

She knew more than him, then. Deangelo still wasn't sure how he'd allowed everything he'd spent the last twelve years building to be swept away in just a few hours, even if it was temporary. 'You do?'

'Everything has changed. For both of us. That's confusing how we relate to each other, how we interact.'

'So this right now is just confusion?'

She laughed. 'Maybe. No, definitely. But I think we're two of a kind, you and I. We don't allow ourselves what comes so naturally to others, for different reasons probably, but still. I want to change that, I want to start living like everyone else. To stop being afraid to reach out for what I want. And tonight…' She swallowed. 'Tonight I want you. I'm not looking for more. Good God, I don't think I could handle more, not from someone

as intense as you. I need training wheels for
a little while longer; I'm very out of practice
when it comes to relationships. So I have no
expectations, except that tomorrow things
revert to normal. But we've a while until
tomorrow. And I'd like to spend that while
with you…'

Deangelo couldn't imagine the courage
it must have taken to be so very honest, to
be so very vulnerable, and his lack of wor-
thiness, his inability to be so open hit him.
'Are you sure?'

'Unless you've changed your mind.'

'No,' he said hoarsely. 'I should, I think,
but no.'

'Good.' And now it was Harriet's turn
to take his hand. 'I was hoping that's what
you'd say.'

Stopping to draw her back into his arms,
Deangelo banished the doubts still lurking
in his mind with another kiss, her ardent response a welcome reminder that this was
a two-way sudden attraction. Harriet was
right. Tomorrow would take care of itself—
and tonight? Tonight was up to them.

CHAPTER EIGHT

HARRIET WAS USUALLY awake with the dawn, trained into early rising by the need to be up before her father and then by the early start demanded by Deangelo's timetable. But, it turned out, Deangelo was an earlier riser still. And when she finally stirred it was to find Deangelo already dressed, seated by the side of the bed.

'What time is it?' she managed to say, her voice embarrassingly croaky with sleep. It would have been easier to wake up alone, or for him to occupy the now cool place beside her, but this halfway house put her at a disadvantage. To look at him, she would have assumed that Deangelo had slept for eight peaceful hours. He was already dressed in blue chinos and a crisp white shirt, the most formal of the informal clothes they'd purchased, his hair still wet from the shower.

But Harriet knew better. Deangelo had had as much sleep as she had—and that wasn't very much. She pulled the sheets higher, horribly aware of her nakedness, the way she ached deep down, that mixture of satiation and too much. Last night had in every way been too much.

And she, uncharacteristically confident, had loved every sensuous moment. She'd never known sex could be like that, so tender one moment, so fiery the next, pushing her on and on until she wasn't sure where she ended and he began and she didn't care. For the first time in a long time she'd felt that the exaggerated curves of her hips and breasts weren't too much but just right, her fifties hourglass shape fitted into Brazil, fitted into Deangelo's muscled breadth, perfectly.

'It's just past eight. Breakfast is ordered. I'd like to go over our notes during it. Can you be ready in twenty minutes?'

And good morning to you too, Harriet managed not to say, rising onto one arm and pushing the tangle of hair out of her eyes.

'Of course,' she said easily. 'Can you pass me a robe?' She lay watching him as he strode across the room to collect the silk robe she'd bought just two days ago, but when he returned he didn't hand it to her; instead he stood there frowning. Harriet eased herself into a sitting position, sheet high across her chest. She knew what was coming. The talk.

Harriet had been totally honest last night when she'd said she didn't want a relationship with Deangelo. She had such a long way to go to find out who she was when she wasn't spending every moment worrying about her father. She had a business to build. Single-minded, taciturn, control freak billionaires were in no way part of her plan. Last night wasn't her life's purpose, wonderful as it had been, just a memory in the making, so when she looked back she didn't see a grey, solitary, dull existence but glints of fire and adventure.

'Thank you for ordering breakfast.'

For the first time since she'd known him, Deangelo looked disconcerted. 'You're welcome.'

'And thank you for last night. The dancing and, well, everything.' She smiled up at him. 'I know how important today is, and I know what last night was. You don't need to worry. I don't expect you to suddenly be magically in love with me and I'm not magically in love with you—it was just two people exploring an attraction. Maybe a goodbye in a way.'

'Yes.'

'So, if you want me to be ready in twenty minutes you'd better give me some privacy.' She smiled again. 'I promise not to take too long.'

'Right. Okay.' His eyes flicked to the sheet covering her and for one millisecond Harriet could have sworn that his gaze heated up, but immediately his habitual blank expression was right back in place. 'I'll see you soon.'

She breathed a sigh of relief as he handed her the robe and turned and left. So much better for her to deliver the *about last night* speech rather than receive it—and she was a sensible grown-up woman who was not going to feel disappointed that he hadn't argued for a continuance.

It didn't take Harriet too long to shower, quickly washing her hair, bundling it, still damp, into a loose chignon, smoothing on tinted moisturiser, mascara and a little lipstick. She pulled a face as she surveyed her fresh-faced milkmaid wholesomeness in the mirror; she definitely didn't look sophisticated enough to be a naïve but rich investor's wife, but she'd never got the hang of a five-minute full makeover. Her outfit would have to talk for her. She opted for wide silky trousers in navy blue with a white and gold pattern, partnering them with a loose gold vest top, layering up the gold bangles Amber had assured her would make the outfit, and slipping her feet into the kind of wedges that made her relieved that Deangelo usually got chauffeured everywhere.

Exactly twenty minutes later she left the bedroom. The heavy velvet curtains had been pulled back and the French doors opened, allowing the morning light to flood into the overly ornate room. Deangelo was seated at the small table in the dining alcove, his laptop open, ignoring the food spread out before him. An ache in her stomach reminded Harriet that she'd only eaten a couple of the small cheese rolls, some grilled vegetables and prawns last night.

'This looks amazing.'

Deangelo looked up. Had he really been so lost in work he hadn't heard her approach? Was he really as cool as he appeared? It didn't matter, she reminded herself; they had made an agreement. The sort Deangelo always made—brief companionship with no expectations on either side. Harriet just had to act like one of the sophisticated women he usually dated.

'Is that coffee?' she continued in the same overly bright voice. 'Excellent. I need something to wake me up.' At that exact moment she remembered just why she was so tired—and, judging by the heat flaring in Deangelo's eyes as he looked up, he was having exactly the same memories. Cheeks burning, Harriet slipped into the empty chair. The food looked incredible. Whatever the hotel's failings, the kitchen clearly wasn't one of them: freshly baked bread rolls were heaped into a basket, an array of cheeses, meats, jams and fresh fruit spread out on attractive platters, joined by pots of yogurt and a jug of fruit juice. Harriet accepted a cup of milky coffee gratefully, before piling her plate high. Deangelo, she noted, had a few slices of papaya and a black coffee. She looked down at her own teetering pile of food ruefully.

'My sisters are like you. Food to them is a necessity they barely tolerate. Growing up, they were always a little scathing about my appetite. I used to try and eat like they did, then sneak food later. Silly really. I just wanted to be like them, for them to take notice of me in a good way. To include me, as if they were ever going to want to hang out with a half-sister a decade younger.'

She was surprised to see Deangelo's forehead crease as if in pain and stopped abruptly, roll still in hand. 'I'm sorry; you don't need to know this.'

'Half-siblings can be very cruel.' There was a chilling note to his voice and foreboding shivered down Harriet's spine. His face straightened, his expression resolute.

'I'd like to say unthinking rather than cruel.' She stared at her plate. Part of her still hoped that one day Emma and Jayne would act like real sisters. Even after they'd excluded her from their weddings, failed to tell her when nieces and nephews were born, sent Christmas cards to their father only. Even as their visits became more and more infrequent as their father's illness progressed, after they stopped taking her calls and ignored her pleas for help. It wasn't just their financial help she'd wanted. It was their input. For someone else to make the difficult decisions, to reassure her she was doing the right thing. For someone to care.

But someone had. While he still could. Even amidst his own grief, her father had helped her cope with the loss of her mother in every way he could. 'After Mum died I just couldn't eat at all. For weeks. Then one day Dad took me out to Mum's favourite Italian. Nothing fancy, one of those family-run restaurants that are a staple of every small town. The kind where they ply you with garlic bread as soon as you sit down, where every portion could actually feed a family, where they insist you try pudding. And he reminded me that eating together brought Mum more happiness than anything. That cooking together was her favourite pastime.'

Why on earth had she told him all that when the time for confidences was at an end?

'My mother loved to cook too.'

She stilled, barely daring to look at him. She'd never heard Deangelo speak about any member of his family before.

'And she always said breakfast was the most important meal of the day, that you never knew when you'd next get the time or money to eat.' Deangelo said nothing else, but he did add a roll and some cheese to his plate.

Harriet continued to eat automatically, turning that comment over and over in her and she didn't know if it was because of the night they had just shared or the meeting they were preparing for. She suspected a little of both; either way it unnerved her. He usually seemed so impenetrable, but then even superheroes had their vulnerabilities, as Achilles had found out in the end. Coming back to Rio was obviously his. The night they'd shared was because of that weakness, not instead of. No wonder he wanted to pretend it had never happened. The sooner she felt the same the better.

But as she turned to look back at him she couldn't help wishing for a little of last night's courage, for the right to take him in her arms, to thank him for the rings, to wipe away the sadness that still lingered in his eyes. She didn't know what his reasons for being here were, but she hoped that whatever he planned would set him free. He deserved love, as did she. Maybe last night was the first step they both needed.

But part of her wished they could take the next step together.

She bit her lip, pushing the traitorous thought away. Maybe sex had addled her brain. She'd better ensure strict boundaries or the next two weeks or she'd start naming

head. It suggested poverty, not knowing when or where the next meal was coming from.

And the past tense hadn't escaped her either. He'd lost his mother, too. Empathy ached within her, but she didn't know what to say, whether any gesture would be welcomed, last night's intimacy muddying the waters between them, making reaching out to another human being an unwelcome overture rather than a gesture of sympathy.

Neither spoke for the next few minutes. Harriet's appetite had deserted her and she picked at her breakfast, grateful for the bitter coffee. It wasn't until she pushed her plate away that Deangelo looked up again. He picked up a small parcel that lay beside his laptop and handed it to her.

'These arrived this morning; they should be the right size.'

Opening the padded envelope cautiously, she drew out a turquoise ring box and her stomach tumbled with a mixture of fear and anticipation. She'd always dreamt of receiving a box like this, maybe on a moonlit evening by the sea. Never over an awkward breakfast in order to perpetuate a charade.

'I said not to…'

'No one would believe a bride wouldn't wear her wedding ring. Open it.'

With a doubtful glance at him she did, her gasp as much delight as shock as she took in the twisted platinum band and delicate sapphire ring, obviously designed to fit together. They were beautiful. Too beautiful. She'd much rather have worn a huge diamond solitaire or something else not to her taste than the exact same rings she would have picked out for herself.

'These are too much. What if I lost them…?'

'It's no matter.' And of course it wasn't. Deangelo could buy rings like this for every single one of his employees and not even notice. That didn't make it seem right though.

'What about you?'

But he simply shrugged. 'Not all men wear rings.'

'I would never marry someone who didn't want to wear a ring.'

'Then it's a good thing this is not a real marriage. Come on, Harriet, see if they fit. We have a lot to go through.'

Gone was the tender, considerate lover, gone her usually courteous boss. Deangelo's lips pressed tightly together, his forehead pinched with what she assumed was rarely

seen annoyance. Harriet gingerly lifted the rings out of the box, swallowing as she held the engagement ring up, admiring the etchings of leaves decorating the delicate band. This was no standard ring. It was *the* ring.

The perfect gift, just like the coat, just like the library subscription. Only this wasn't a gift she could keep and receiving it just made melancholy settle over her. It seemed so wrong that the person who knew her best was the person who would no longer be in her life. The person who lived a life pretty much devoid of any human warmth and liked it that way.

Silence stretched as she slid first the twisted platinum band and then the sapphir ring onto the fourth finger of her left han Of course they fitted perfectly.

'Do you like them?'

'I love them,' she half whispered. 'I'll care of them.'

He waved away her assurance as if tered not at all.

Unease sat heavily on her and stood up, needing to put some dis tween herself and the food.

Some distance between her gelo. He was such a stranger th

head. It suggested poverty, not knowing when or where the next meal was coming from.

And the past tense hadn't escaped her either. He'd lost his mother, too. Empathy ached within her, but she didn't know what to say, whether any gesture would be welcomed, last night's intimacy muddying the waters between them, making reaching out to another human being an unwelcome overture rather than a gesture of sympathy.

Neither spoke for the next few minutes. Harriet's appetite had deserted her and she picked at her breakfast, grateful for the bitter coffee. It wasn't until she pushed her plate away that Deangelo looked up again. He picked up a small parcel that lay beside his laptop and handed it to her.

'These arrived this morning; they should be the right size.'

Opening the padded envelope cautiously, she drew out a turquoise ring box and her stomach tumbled with a mixture of fear and anticipation. She'd always dreamt of receiving a box like this, maybe on a moonlit evening by the sea. Never over an awkward breakfast in order to perpetuate a charade.

'I said not to...'

'No one would believe a bride wouldn't wear her wedding ring. Open it.'

With a doubtful glance at him she did, her gasp as much delight as shock as she took in the twisted platinum band and delicate sapphire ring, obviously designed to fit together. They were beautiful. Too beautiful. She'd much rather have worn a huge diamond solitaire or something else not to her taste than the exact same rings she would have picked out for herself.

'These are too much. What if I lost them…?'

'It's no matter.' And of course it wasn't. Deangelo could buy rings like this for every single one of his employees and not even notice. That didn't make it seem right though.

'What about you?'

But he simply shrugged. 'Not all men wear rings.'

'I would never marry someone who didn't want to wear a ring.'

'Then it's a good thing this is not a real marriage. Come on, Harriet, see if they fit. We have a lot to go through.'

Gone was the tender, considerate lover, gone her usually courteous boss. Deangelo's lips pressed tightly together, his forehead pinched with what she assumed was rarely seen annoyance. Harriet gingerly lifted the rings out of the box, swallowing as she held the engagement ring up, admiring the etchings of leaves decorating the delicate band. This was no standard ring. It was *the* ring.

The perfect gift, just like the coat, just like the library subscription. Only this wasn't a gift she could keep and receiving it just made melancholy settle over her. It seemed so wrong that the person who knew her best was the person who would no longer be in her life. The person who lived a life pretty much devoid of any human warmth and liked it that way.

Silence stretched as she slid first the twisted platinum band and then the sapphire ring onto the fourth finger of her left hand. Of course they fitted perfectly.

'Do you like them?'

'I love them,' she half whispered. 'I'll take care of them.'

He waved away her assurance as if it mattered not at all.

Unease sat heavily on her and Harriet stood up, needing to put some distance between herself and the food.

Some distance between her and Deangelo. He was such a stranger this morning, and she didn't know if it was because of the night they had just shared or the meeting they were preparing for. She suspected a little of both; either way it unnerved her. He usually seemed so impenetrable, but then even superheroes had their vulnerabilities, as Achilles had found out in the end. Coming back to Rio was obviously his. The night they'd shared was because of that weakness, not instead of. No wonder he wanted to pretend it had never happened. The sooner she felt the same the better.

But as she turned to look back at him she couldn't help wishing for a little of last night's courage, for the right to take him in her arms, to thank him for the rings, to wipe away the sadness that still lingered in his eyes. She didn't know what his reasons for being here were, but she hoped that whatever he planned would set him free. He deserved love, as did she. Maybe last night was the first step they both needed.

But part of her wished they could take the next step together.

She bit her lip, pushing the traitorous thought away. Maybe sex had addled her brain. She'd better ensure strict boundaries for the next two weeks or she'd start naming imaginary children and picking out dream homes…

'Right—' she was relieved to hear her voice sound so steady '—let's get to work. We have an hour before the meeting; what do you need me to do?'

The initial meeting was to start off in the lobby. The three Caetano siblings had offered a tour of the grand-if-decaying hotel before taking the formalities up to the boardroom. Harriet could feel the butterflies tumbling through her stomach as the lift took them back down to the lobby. She'd sat through hundreds of high-powered business meetings in her time with Aion, many involving much higher stakes monetarily than this, but it was clear this particular deal had nothing to do with money. How could it? It was a terrible investment.

Deangelo was tense as he stood next to her, his hands curled into white-knuckled fists, a muscle beating in his jaw. He looked dangerous, more like a prize fighter than a newly rich businessman, and Harriet, steeling herself, slipped her hand into his. 'We're meant to be on honeymoon, remember?'

Taking his hand wasn't purely about their

charade. A casual observer might detect no emotion in Deangelo, but Harriet had never seen him so preternaturally still, apart from that one muscle, as if he was concealing some strong emotion, not, as she often thought, a stranger to it.

Whoever these Caetanos were, there was history here. Personal history. History worth spending a great deal of money and time on.

Deangelo didn't respond as she took a firmer grip of his hand, stiller than she'd ever thought any human could be, until the lift doors opened, revealing the marble lobby beyond. In that moment it was as if he'd flicked a switch, turning himself on, as he strode out of the lift, towing Harriet alongside. His smile was wider than she'd ever seen it, eyes beaming with a frank bonhomie as he slipped an arm around Harriet's shoulders and held her close.

'Senhor and Senhorita Caetano? *Ola*, I'm Marcos Santos and this, this is my beautiful bride, Harriet.' His accent was thicker than usual, and subtly different. A regional accent, she assumed. 'Thank you so much for agreeing to meet me, and thank you for the beautiful suite. It's really made our honeymoon perfect, hasn't it, *querida*?'

Harriet forced a matching smile onto her own face. 'Oh, yes, it's lovely.'

'It's okay if we use English?' he asked. 'My wife—' he squeezed her shoulder proprietarily, and her body jumped to attention, the memory of his touch still imprinted in every nerve '—my wife, she doesn't speak Portuguese.'

The Caetano trio turned to look directly at Harriet as he spoke and she stifled a gasp of shock as they did so. The siblings were all a good fifteen years older than Deangelo, but there was no escaping the similarities in the shape of their eyes, the strong jawline. The arrogant set of all four pairs of shoulders. Maybe a casual observer wouldn't see the resemblance—Deangelo was taller and broader, his hair curled, his mouth wider, his nose more Roman, eyes amber rather than brown. But she knew every inch of him and could see where the similarities overlapped as if laid out on a map.

She'd known this deal was personal, as personal as it could get. She should have known that meant family.

Another squeeze on her shoulder reminded her of her role in this soap opera and she hastily pinned the smile back onto her face, hoping the shock and recognition didn't show in her eyes. There was no answering recognition in the avaricious smiles greeting them, but maybe they saw simply what they wanted to see.

She held out a hand automatically. 'No Portuguese yet. Marcos keeps promising to teach me, but we've just not had a chance. It's all been such a whirlwind.' She forced a giggle.

As introductions continued, Harriet covertly studied the Caetanos, aware that she was being studied in turn. Isabela Caetano was making no secret of her comprehensive summing up and Harriet was relieved that Amber had insisted that she be kitted out so thoroughly. The glamorous older woman would have instantly noted a high street bag or cheap shoes; as it was, her gaze lingered disdainfully on Harriet's rough and ready chignon, her own hair perfectly styled to match her fully made-up face and manicured nails. Her deceptively simple dress was obviously, even to Harriet's inexperienced eyes, haute couture, fitting every dramatic curve perfectly. Her brothers were no less expensively dressed, whereas she and Deangelo were in showy designer labels that screamed money but lacked the old-world class the Caetanos wore as if they had been born to it.

Somehow Harriet managed to keep up her bubbly, if a little naïve and aspirational, persona during the rest of the introductions, making small talk about her first impressions of Rio de Janeiro and how it compared to London and New York. But while she smiled and chatted her mind continued to whirl, adding two and two over and over again but never quite managing to make four. Was she looking at Deangelo's cousins? His uncles and aunt? Why did they not know who he was? Why the secrecy? Did the Caetanos really not see the predator behind the mask? See their own features mirrored in his smile?

Before the day was done she would have answers, whether Deangelo wanted to tell her or not.

The morning went as flawlessly as planned, the Caetanos so busy trying to impress them that they didn't take any time to assess the situation, just as Deangelo had predicted. This was no gamble. It was the execution of a well-honed plan and all the sweeter for it.

The only time he had stumbled was when Bruno's gaze had lingered on the scar bisecting his left cheek. Deangelo didn't know whether he was more relieved or angry when his gaze had moved swiftly on. Did Bruno not remember inflicting such a scar? Had Deangelo really been so far below him that he had no memory of the brutal assault? But he remembered clearly how the older man had turned his back the second the whip descended, not caring about what damage he had inflicted or where.

He'd care soon enough.

The tour of the hotel was heavy on prestige and history if light on detail; likewise, the portfolio of other properties in the Caetano empire showcased the symbolism of their name, interspersed with the glossy new resorts developed by Isabela. It was easy to see where the money had gone. Deangelo had barely had a chance to look at the portfolio before the contract was produced. It had already been to both sets of lawyers, this meeting just a formality. Deangelo made a show of flicking through it, aware of the hunger beneath the Caetanos' smiles, the concern and curiosity in Harriet's eyes, the trembling in his own hand as he lifted the heavy fountain pen and stared at the X awaiting just his signature.

This was it. He was not about to make himself part of the family business, whether his siblings wanted him there or not. He was about to become the majority shareholder. The illegitimate street rat was about to be the new Chairman of the Board and they had no idea.

He glanced up at their wide, disingenuous smiles, no doubt gloating as they fleeced the naïve investor for three times what the shares were worth. If they'd just agreed to pay his mother's medical bills that day. If they hadn't literally thrown him out, taking a riding crop to him as they had done so, then he wouldn't be here right now.

But they had and he was.

Deangelo signed *LDM Santos*, the looping script making the initials hard to read.

He pushed the contract over to Bruno, who barely glanced at Deangelo's signature before scrawling his own.

The deal was done. He'd won.

The meeting ended with an offer to send the new shareholder and his bride to one of the new island resorts for a week: an offer Deangelo smilingly accepted.

He needed time to regroup, time to talk to his lawyer and start to put in motion the second part of the plan, which would be implemented at the shareholders' meeting in a couple of weeks. The Caetanos might have realised by then that they had managed to hand over more than fifty per cent of the company, but they would have no idea that they had handed all the power into the hands of one man. He couldn't wait to see the self-satisfied smirks wiped off their faces for good.

Maybe then he would actually feel something. Because right now he still felt numb. As numb as he'd felt the day his mother died, as numb as he'd felt every day since, driven by nothing but cold revenge. The only time he hadn't felt numb was last night.

Last night… He'd lost control and that was unacceptable, especially now, with everything he'd worked for at his fingertips. There was no time for any kind of emotion, not until his siblings were stripped of everything they held dear: their inheritance, their position in society, their good name. Maybe that day he would finally be free.

Harriet said nothing after they'd said their goodbyes and walked back to the lift and to their suite, her thoughtful expression giving little away. She unlocked the door, preceding him into the suite's sitting room, walking straight over to where the French doors were still unlocked, letting the slight sea breeze into the room. She stood with her back to him, looking out towards the sea.

Her shoulders straightened as she inhaled. 'You should have told me,' she said at last.

He didn't need to ask what. 'There was no reason for you to know. You're not here as my guest, Harriet. You're an employee.' Was he reminding her or himself? He strode over to the sideboard and poured some water. 'Here.'

She turned, accepting the glass he held out to her. 'Yes, I am aware of that.' If he'd hurt her with his casual dismissal of last night and all they'd shared she didn't show it. 'I know I'm here because you trust me to do a good job. You trust me so much that you are paying me well over the odds for me to be here...'

He held up a hand dismissively. 'I have more money than anyone can comprehend. The price was irrelevant.'

'Maybe. But you still wanted me by your side for this deal, not because I was the right person to act as your bride—although I am probably the only person you can trust to keep quiet, to not run to the press, but because I am damn good at my job, at looking out for your interests. But your secrets are stopping me from doing that, from doing my job properly. I'm not prepared. If I'd known that the Caetanos were your family…'

'What? What would you have done differently? Because, make no mistake, Harriet, those people back there? They are not my family.'

She stared. 'Of course they are! I can't believe they couldn't see it; it was almost blindingly obvious.'

'You said it yourself—you left Aion to make a family. Families are forged, not made just because we're unlucky enough to share blood with people.'

Harriet flushed, folding her arms as she confronted him. 'I did say it. But you know what? It doesn't matter. Because I don't see you forging anything, not one human relationship at any time in the whole time I've known you. All you forge is more money. What's it all for, Deangelo? What use is all the money in the world if you're all alone?'

It took everything he'd worked at over the

last twelve years to stay completely still, to not betray any emotion even though every word she spoke struck him with deadly aim, striking straight through the armour he'd encased himself in, the armour he'd thought was impenetrable, causing physical pain.

'Some of us deserve to be alone, Harriet,' he bit out.

Her eyes softened. 'No one deserves that, Deangelo.'

He stabbed at his chest, contempt dripping from every pore. 'You think money and handmade suits and private jets make a person worthwhile?'

'No, of course not.'

'You want to know what's under this veneer? You want to know who Deangelo Santos is? He doesn't exist. He's a fake.'

'What do you mean?'

'Deangelo's my middle name. My mother called me by it sometimes. It means from the angel. She used it when she wanted me to know she loved me, no matter what, that she didn't regret having me, no matter what. For eighteen years I was Luciano Deangelo Marcos Santos. But I left Luciano behind me when I moved to London.'

'Why?' She took a step closer.

'Why? Because Luciano was a nothing. He was a no-good street rat. A boy who couldn't save his dying mother, whose failure was carved into his face, who has to stare at it every damn day. A man who deserves that reminder. Who deserves to remember that he came from nothing. That he is nothing. That he failed.'

Harriet didn't move for a long moment and then she took one long step until she stood next to him, and then her arms were around him, holding his unyielding body close. 'That's not true,' she whispered. 'No one is nothing, that boy wasn't nothing, the man isn't nothing. Let me in, Deangelo. Let me help.'

He stood still, trying to ignore her soft curves pressed against him, trying to keep numb. Feeling nothing protected him; it always had. This simmering heat, this need igniting in his veins made him vulnerable. And yet he stayed as Harriet pressed even closer, trailing kisses along his jaw, swift and sweet and tantalising.

'Let me help,' she said again and oh, God, she was so warm, so alive. She was comfort and life and when he'd been with her last night he'd managed to feel, to forget. Dangerous. And so, so seductive, just like her touch, those light kisses.

With a smothered curse Deangelo captured Harriet's hand in his, tilting her chin with his other hand, gazing at her lush mouth and half-closed eyes with a mixture of helplessness and need. Now was the time to step away; they'd established the rules last night and he never broke the rules.

But he was back in Rio and he'd been a very different person here—and that young man who had everything to prove was still imprisoned inside him; somehow here the walls were thinner, the distinctions blurred.

'Show me,' Harriet said softly, her gaze burning into him, and Deangelo knew he couldn't stop now, not while she was willing him on. He slid his hand round to the nape of her neck, trailing his fingers along her jawline as he did so, splaying his hand wide as he finally gave in to her plea, to the demands of his body and, lowering his head, captured her mouth with his. Her soft moan of satisfaction was all he needed, deepening the kiss ruthlessly, demandingly, knowing she matched him in every way, her hands raking through his hair, down his back.

Revenge was there waiting for him. Let

it wait for now. He had the rest of his life to enjoy what he'd put in motion today. Right now there was sensation and heat and, most intoxicating of all, there was hope.

CHAPTER NINE

RIO WAS TURNING out to be more of an adventure than Harriet could ever have anticipated. Over the last few days the mornings had been reserved for work, the afternoons for exploring. Harriet had tried to surf on Ipanema beach, taken the cable car to Sugarloaf Mountain and wandered through the Jardin Botanico. In the evenings they danced until late, returning to the hotel to make love. There was no talk about stopping—just as there was no talk about the future—an unspoken agreement that all rules and plans were to be put aside for this brief spell.

But today was different. Deangelo had mentioned over breakfast that he was planning to visit his aunt and that Harriet was welcome to accompany him if she chose. He'd sounded offhand, as if her decision meant nothing either way, but Harriet was learning to read him and the tightness around his mouth and the muscle beating in his cheek indicated that he did, in fact, care very much.

She hugged that knowledge to herself. She was wanted and needed and even if it was short-term it was glorious. She was living the charade and she was loving it.

It was more than the fun of being a tourist, more than the sex; it was the companionship. The feeling that she understood and was understood in turn. The only cloud was the secrets she didn't quite dare to pry into. She still didn't know how or when Deangelo's mother had died and why he took all the blame on himself or where the Caetanos fitted in. Maybe today would provide some answers.

But maybe it was better for Deangelo's secrets to remain just that, because their existence was a barrier between them, a reminder that, no matter how much fun they were having, it wasn't real.

Walking back into the sitting room, she saw Deangelo standing, staring out of the window, expression utterly inscrutable.

'Hi,' she said. 'I'm ready.'

He turned, eyes darkening to gold as he

looked her up and down in a way that made Harriet feel as if her clothes were utterly transparent. One thing was clear; in the unlikely event he ever tried to hire her again, she would never be able to accept. And as Deangelo didn't do relationships, once this trip was over their paths would part for good. She couldn't help a pang of regret at the thought.

But it was done—and she had been equally culpable in instigating the shift in their relationship.

'Are your shoes comfortable?'

She blinked. That was probably the last thing she'd expected him to say. 'Yes. I think so.'

'Good. We have some walking to do. Keep your bag close. You don't have any valuables in it?'

'Work phone and card and a lipstick.'

'The phone's encrypted?'

'Of course.'

'If anyone tries to take your bag, let them. Okay. Let's go.'

'Okay. I thought we were visiting your family.'

His expression didn't change. 'We are.'

Deangelo barely spoke again until they

were in the taxi. The sun shone bright with mid-afternoon intensity and the beach and pavements seemed to have taken on a sleepy quality as sun haze mixed with the pollution to produce a shimmering curtain that dulled and slowed the passing scene.

'The Caetanos live in the other direction,' he said at last. 'Past Ipanema and out to the outskirts. They live in the kind of area where the city is like a distant dream, where the rich don't worry about rubbing shoulders with the people who clean their houses and streets. They live in an estate patrolled by security guards, on a street where pampered young *senhors* and *senhoritas* are chauffeured in air-conditioned cars to private schools and exclusive beach clubs so that they too can grow up believing themselves masters of all they can see.'

'Is that where you grew up?'

He'd alluded to poverty and she'd seen its scars in his eyes. But at the same time Deangelo was so at home with his wealth; it didn't seem newly won. Not for him gaudy trimmings or ostentatious displays. Even his watch was discreet: the best Swiss engineering presented in a neat grey package. Tasteful and the very best engineering and craftsmanship. A sneak thief would probably pass it by, but it cost twice as much as the diamond-covered branded watches favoured by the Caetano brothers.

'I grew up there, but I'm not from there.'

He retreated into silence and after a while Harriet turned her attention to the window, watching Rio live and breathe as the car inched its way through busy, noisy traffic away from the beach and into the heart of the bustling, vibrant city. The minutes ticked away but she barely noticed, caught up in the sights and sounds. Eventually the taxi began to make its way up one of the city's steep iconic hills, the traffic lessening as they progressed. The neighbourhood felt very different to Copacabana, the faded mansions and old houses giving the impression of a once fashionable area in decline, although there were enough signs of refurbishment to suggest some regeneration, a suggestion confirmed by the boutique hotels and art galleries they passed as they continued their journey, the trendy little cafés rubbing shoulders with older, shabbier bars.

'This is cool,' she said. 'It makes me think of how Chelsea must have been in the sixties, before it totally gentrified and big money took over.'

'Santa Teresa? Yes, there are parallels.'

Harriet remembered his offhand comment on their first evening that he thought she would like to stay here. She noted a quirky antique shop. He was right. Which once again begged the question—how did he know her so well when for three years he had barely seemed to notice her at all?

At that moment the car pulled up in front of a pink mansion surrounded by vibrant gardens and Deangelo paid the taxi driver before exiting the car, Harriet following suit, joining him outside the imposing wooden gates. 'What a beautiful house.'

'This was built by Marcos Caetano in the nineteenth century. Only one generation actually lived here; my great-great-grandfather joined the exile of the well-heeled to the outer edges of the city, my father moved yet again. But this was where the family empire was built.'

'And now?' She sensed there was much more going on here than some retelling of old family history.

'Now? Now it belongs to me. I bought it five years ago. Anonymously, of course.'

'To you? But you never come here!' Not that it mattered. Deangelo could probably afford a home in every city in the world if he so chose. But in a city where so many had nothing it seemed obscene to own an empty house.

Although, the more she looked, the more signs of life she saw. The gates weren't locked, just closed, and the house looked lived in, signs tacked neatly to outside walls, the formal path running to the front door maintained.

Deangelo raised a surprised brow. 'I don't need to come here. It's a training centre, for teens and young people from the neighbouring *favelas*.'

Of course it was. And another piece was added to the jigsaw that made up this intriguing man—only every time she slotted in a new piece the jigsaw trebled in size. 'What kind of training centre?'

'Hospitality. It's a budget hotel, and runs like any other hotel except here most of the staff are being trained and that, of course, is reflected in the price.'

'What a great idea.' Harriet smiled brightly, trying to bury her shock. How hadn't she known he was involved in an initiative like this? She'd spent three years handling his correspondence, managing his inbox and yet she'd had no idea. Oh, he was philanthropic, but in a hands-off way. Cheques written and sent, all invitations to gala events declined. But this was personal in every way, located as it was in the house belonging to the family he was trying to destroy. His family.

'I started out funding schools and places at university, I still do, but that kind of study isn't for everyone. This place gives kids a chance; it's not easy to find legitimate employment when you come from the undocumented side of town. We provide training, work experience, first here and then later in other establishments, more specialised to individual skills. We offer maths and languages for those who need or want them, business studies, too. We then help them find their first job.'

'And now,' she teased, 'you own a whole chain of hotels to provide that extra training!'

But her smile wasn't answered, his forehead creasing as if he were trying to find the answer to an insoluble riddle. 'I suppose I have,' he said slowly. 'I hadn't considered that side of things. Come on.'

With that he pushed open the gate and strode into the front garden, Harriet a step behind. As they neared the front door it opened. They were clearly expected, lines of young adults in neat uniforms waiting to greet them like something out of a country house drama. At the front, wreathed in smiles, stood a young woman with abundant hair coiled into a complicated knot and a man of Deangelo's own age who greeted him with a shout of delight and a complicated handshake followed by much backslapping. Harriet stared. She'd never seen Deangelo so relaxed, a smile so warm and real on the usually stern face.

'This is Harriet,' he said at last in English.

Just Harriet. Not 'my PA.' Not 'my fake wife.' Just her name. Even so, the glances the pair flashed her way were frankly curious and Harriet was glad she'd left her new rings in the safe in the hotel.

'Harriet, I'd like you to meet my cousins, Milena and Luis. They run the hotel for me.'

She smiled, but her hands shook as she accepted their welcome embrace. Deangelo was letting her in, showing her who he was and where he came from.

This could change everything, if Harriet

was just brave enough to let it. If she could admit to herself that she wanted him, too. Wanted him. It had been so long since Harriet had thought about what *she* wanted, put her happiness first, the agency her first tentative steps towards a future she chose. Falling for someone as intense, as troubled, as enigmatic as Deangelo could derail all her plans.

But as she looked at the welcoming smiles of Deangelo's cousins, looked behind them at the gleaming paintwork and lovingly polished wood in the hotel entrance hall, the pride and dignity of the assembled staff, ready to show off their hard work to the man who made it his mission to provide them with a future, she knew it might already be too late. It wasn't just the sex, the hormones flooding through her newly awakened body, that was the issue here. It was the man who had awakened her.

Let me in, she'd asked just a few days ago. And here he was doing exactly that, or as close to that as he could possibly get. Deangelo glanced over at Harriet as she chatted to Milena and Luis, her face alive with interest and curiosity during the tour of the hotel.

'This half is very simple, more a hostel than a hotel,' Milena explained. 'The students start out here, learning to deal with simple bookings and queries, to prepare buffet meals and snacks. Then, after six months, they move to the other side, which operates as a boutique hotel. Some know by this point whether they prefer the kitchens or hospitality, others are still not sure.'

'It's such a good idea.' Harriet stopped to peek into one of the pristine family rooms. 'I much prefer this to where we're staying, and I love that the tourists get to give back to the community as well.'

'That's Deangelo for you,' Luis said. 'So many schemes, but nothing is just given away. Everything he does is designed to get people to help themselves, whether it's the university scholarships or the schools and childcare or the community centres...'

'That's enough.' Deangelo interrupted his cousin. 'Harriet doesn't need to hear all about this stuff.'

'Oh, but I do,' she said. 'So there are classrooms here on site?'

'Yes, at the back. Practical classrooms— kitchens and a workshop. But also language labs. We try and make sure as many leave here with reasonable English as possible, others also add Spanish and French. The more languages they have, the more employable they are, the more opportunities they have.'

Deangelo was as interested in the tour as Harriet; he might have designed the hotel but this was his first visit. It was incredible, seeing his concept made flesh.

It was the only tangible thing he felt was his. His entire empire was built on shifting networks and clouds. On third parties and their needs for his technology. Whether car sharing or restaurant finding or holiday booking or room letting—he facilitated millions of exchanges every single day, but he owned none of them. There was nothing he could look at and say 'This is mine,' The office block he owned and lived in had been designed by someone else; it was a place of utility, that was all. Not of passion.

Possessions didn't motivate him. He didn't dream of a home or a family. He didn't deserve such things. But he provided thousands of jobs all over the globe and he was making a difference right here in Brazil. Maybe that would be enough on Judgement Day.

But this hotel was filled with passion and pride, not least from his cousins: Luis, whose footballing dreams had crashed and burned like so many thousands of other not-quite-talented-enough boys, leaving his future uncertain, and Milena, widowed too young, left with two small children and no income. He could have housed and supported them without even noticing the spend; instead he had asked them to help him turn his dreams into reality, and in doing so had given them purpose.

The tour ended in the bright sunlit restaurant, tables spilling out onto the flower-filled terrace. Two graduating students served the coffee and delicious little tarts, answering Harriet's questions in near-perfect English as she quizzed them about their futures. Both had jobs lined up, one here in Santa Teresa, in one of the boutique hotels further up in the hills; the other was heading to one of the city's restaurants.

'That is one of the most inspiring things I have ever seen,' Harriet said as they left, promising to return before their visit ended.

'It's nothing.' He shrugged her words off, uncomfortable with her praise, but she shook her head stubbornly.

'It's not nothing. You heard that boy, Paolo, in there. He was living on the street five years ago! On the street. Headed nowhere safe. Now he has an education, a job, a future, and you made that happen.'

'No. He made that happen. I simply provide the place and the opportunity. The rest is down to him.' Her praise made him uncomfortable. It was Luis and Milena and the other staff and teachers who really deserved it; it was the kids themselves, their ability to learn and grow and hope—things Deangelo had never learned despite his degrees and business empire.

He lived locked away. No friends, his family a continent away, no relationships that lasted longer than a few convenient weeks, no ties. Every day he looked in the mirror and his scar would remind him of all he had failed to do. Of who he really was. What he deserved.

But today, visiting the hotel, seeing Harriet's face lit up with interest, seeing his vision come to life, he had felt just a little less of a failure. Every night, Harriet's curves entwined around him, her lips on his, her breathing in time with his, he felt less alone. But he didn't deserve the way he felt with her. And if she knew it all she would agree.

'So where are we going now?' she asked.

'For many tourists the *favelas* are a place to avoid, unless they're on a tour. A few are more sanitised and some tourists even stay there, another tick on their places-to-see list. But many are not safe for strangers, especially strangers with money.'

'Does that mean we're heading to one?'

'It does. But don't worry. You'll be safe with me.'

Her answering smile was unexpected, as was the trust in her eyes. Trust that warmed him even as it warned him to be careful. 'I know.'

It had been twelve years since he'd last walked into the twisty streets of the *favela*, but he still knew his way instinctively. The boys playing football hadn't been born when he'd left, but they had the same hope and determination in their eyes as they tackled each other, performing tricks in the hope some scout might chance by and transform their lives. The old men sitting outside the bar were as familiar as his view from his office window, the noises and smells and vibrancy making his chest ache with a nostalgia he'd thought he'd trained out of himself many years ago.

All the time he was hyperaware of Harriet

by his side, taking everything in, her hand in his, her stride matching his. 'I thought you grew up on the other side of the city,' she said.

'I did.'

'But this is your home, too. Unless you've pioneered some navigation chip and that's beaming directions straight to your brain?'

'Not yet, but good idea. I'll get the tech guys to get started straight away.' He stopped outside a bar, newly opened since he'd left, tables and chairs on the terrace looking out over the spectacular view. 'Drink?'

Harriet nodded and he led her through the brightly painted bar and onto the terrace, ordering a couple of cold beers as he did so.

He looked around, admiring the bright, clean decor, the simple menu scrawled onto a board. 'When I lived here places like this, where outsiders could come, just didn't exist. The way some of the *favelas* have been cleaned up is controversial, and not always long-lasting. That's why everything I do is about changing from within, giving the residents the opportunities they need to change things, and to make sure those changes are what they need, rather than what some politician who has never set foot in these streets thinks they need.'

'Like what?'

He shrugged. 'Education, healthcare, community initiatives, jobs and training. The problem isn't that people aren't always documented, or that the settlements have no infrastructure. It's the lack of opportunity and hope. Every boy out there dreams about being a footballer. That's the way out. When it doesn't happen, and for ninety-nine point nine per cent of them it won't happen, they have no backup plan, and the only future they see is in the gangs. And so the cycle continues. I just want to change that cycle.'

The beers arrived then, with a smile and a message that they were on the house. The owner had recognised him, then? The fund he'd set up to help entrepreneurs fund businesses such as this had proved popular. He took a sip of the tart, icy drink, sitting back, his gaze flitting between the incredible view of the city and the girl opposite. She looked so cool and put together, only her eyes betraying her excitement and her curiosity. 'So how did you end up here?'

'My mother was from here.' He took another drink, weighing his words carefully. Nobody, not even the family who still lived here, knew his whole story. He'd kept it within his whole life, but the urge to unburden himself was almost overwhelming, even knowing that she might turn away if she knew it all.

But she should know just who she was sleeping with, that he was no hero.

'So Luis and Milena are cousins on your mother's side?'

He nodded. 'She was a dancer; she used to frequent dance halls just like the ones I have taken you to. She was so beautiful and so talented; she got a lot of attention, including from my father.'

'Augusto Caetano.' It wasn't a question.

'He was a lot older, with three teenage children and a wife he didn't live with. He offered my mother a job as his housekeeper. It was her chance to get out of the *favela*, to earn money, to live somewhere safe, in beautiful surroundings. She had her own cottage in the grounds of his estate, her own car, could use the pool. She said it was like a dream come true, that she felt like a princess when she first went there. And she didn't have to do much manual work; she managed cleaners and cooks. More like the woman of the house than an employee.'

'Did she love him?'

'I don't know. I think so, by the end. I don't know if she went there knowing he wanted her to be his mistress or if it just happened. But she stayed and a couple of years later she had me; she was only just in her twenties.'

'Did you know Augusto was your father?'

'Not in so many words, but as I grew up it was clear. We still lived in the cottage in the grounds, but I went to an exclusive local school, played tennis and learned to ride. Augusto's wife lived in the countryside—she never came to Rio; he always visited her—but occasionally his other children, his other legitimate children, would come and stay and my mother and I would fade into the background. It was clear that they knew, that they hated us, though.' He picked up his beer, needing to touch something tangible, anchor himself to the here and now. 'I worshipped them. Not so much Isabela—she always had a mean streak—but Bruno and Tiago. They seemed so cool, everything I aspired to be. Occasionally, if they were alone, they might be kinder. As if I were a puppy. Play a game of ball. Once Tiago took me to the beach on his scooter. I spent my life hoping it would happen again.'

'Sounds like your brothers would be good matches for my sisters.'

He smiled at that notion. 'Can you imagine?'

'All too well. So you were what—ten when Augusto died? That's very young. I'm sorry.'

'His death would have been hard enough, but what followed was worse. He'd told my mother that he'd made provision for her, for me. Whether that's true or not I don't know. All I do know is that we were thrown out before the funeral was held. That there was nowhere for us to go apart from back here. No more work for my mother, no more school for me. We belonged nowhere, had nothing. My aunt took us in, in her tiny house, gave us a room to share. I had the bed and my mother the floor. I'm not sure I'll ever forgive myself for that.'

'You were a child.'

'I was ten. Round here that's old enough to grow up, to start being a man. But I was too busy feeling sorry for myself, blaming her for the loss of my life, not knowing how to fit in.' He paused, not wanting to relive those months. 'The only way to survive was to forget all I had been. To play football and run errands for the men, knowing that half the time they were illegal. My mother did her best to get me into school, but I didn't see the point. I think I broke her heart. Young, arrogant, entitled fool.'

Harriet reached across the table and laid her hand on his. 'Don't be so hard on yourself.'

'I deserve it. And more.' He took a deep breath. 'But then she got sick. There are no hospitals here, no doctors we could afford. I knew that Bruno was living back at the family estate so I went there to beg him to help. Despite everything, a part of me still worshipped him, still thought that he might have some feelings for me. I even fantasised that he would offer us our old house, welcome me as a brother. Idiot.'

'I take it that your plan didn't work.' Her eyes flickered to his scar as if she guessed the next step in his sorry saga.

'He told me I was nothing, that my mother was nothing, that we deserved nothing, street rats and vermin that we were. He threw me out, but not before taking his riding crop to me—he gave me this.' He ran his finger down his cheek, feeling the ridged skin underneath. 'Told me he never wanted to see me again, gave me one parting lash; he didn't even wait to see where it landed. I went home with my face torn and empty-handed. I'd failed. And she died a few weeks later.'

'Which is not your fault,' Harriet said fiercely. But he shook his head.

'If I'd not run around with the gangs but found a job, if I'd approached Bruno differently, if I'd noticed she was ill earlier. If I had just let her have the bed…'

'Then maybe nothing would have changed. You can't blame yourself, Deangelo.'

But he could and he did. 'After she died I managed to find a school to take me, then got a scholarship to another, better school, and from there the scholarship to Cambridge. I vowed that I would make sure no other woman or child died in the *favela* because of lack of healthcare, that every child would get an education and a chance to be someone. And I vowed that Bruno Caetano will know exactly what it's like to have his life torn apart and be left with nothing.'

'And then what? Will that make you happy?'

'I don't do happiness,' he said softly. 'It's not in my DNA. Come on, I want to introduce you to my aunt. I think you'll like her.'

'Everyone deserves happiness, Deangelo.

And I think your mother would want you to have that above all else.'

He didn't need absolution, didn't deserve it, but the warmth in her voice, the empathy in her eyes, allowed the first tendrils of something new to start unfurling. Something that felt like a future.

CHAPTER TEN

'You know…' Harriet said as she rubbed more suntan lotion onto her exposed legs. 'I really liked Rio, but I have to say this is paradise. At least, it will be.'

'Really? What's stopping it from being paradise right now? The hammock is maybe not comfortable enough? The ocean views not quite spectacular enough? Your breakfast not prepared exactly to your liking? Book not gripping enough?'

The teasing tone in Deangelo's voice was new, as was the humorous glint in his eyes. Harriet glanced over, her eyes lingering on every exposed muscle and sinew as he lounged on a large sunbed situated next to her hammock. She knew every inch of that body, how it felt, how it tasted. A week after they'd first made love, it still seemed incredible to her that they had reached this place.

So, they hadn't discussed what happened next, what returning to London would mean for this very new, very delicate closeness. There was still a week to go. They'd figure it out.

She swallowed, a little voice warning her that this was all too good to be true. She just wasn't a wanton goddess who lay in hammocks on sun-kissed beaches next to gorgeous men. She was even wearing a bikini, shy as she had been to put on something so revealing, but the light in Deangelo's eyes—and the way he had instantly removed it—had emboldened her and now she walked around without wanting to pull on a cover-up, secure in her skin for the first time in a long time. She loved the confidence he gave her, how desirable he made her feel. As if she could do anything, be anyone. If she could just keep that feeling when she returned to London, it was the greatest gift imaginable.

Turning her thoughts firmly back to Deangelo's question, she tried to articulate what she meant. 'The hotel is perfect in many ways. It's in a lot better shape than the Rio hotel, although it should be, it's so new. The location is amazing and the attention to detail is great, but it doesn't utilise the location properly. We're surrounded by all this amazing wildlife; the hotel should educate and protect, not just use it as a backdrop. Plus, as this place is all-inclusive, it does nothing for the local economy. Visitors should be encouraged to explore, not live in a bubble.'

'Some people like a bubble.'

'True, but this place is half empty. Rebranding it as a wildlife paradise, getting the locals involved and supportive, could transform everything. Differentiate this from all the other identikit beach resorts and transform lives.'

She shifted, enjoying the way the sun saturated her very bones with heat. She'd been surprised when Deangelo had taken up Isabela Caetano's offer of a week in one of her island resorts. Although they had two weeks of little activity between signing the contracts and the first shareholder meeting, vacations just weren't his style. It would have been more usual for him to return to London in the interim; she'd assumed that he would spend the two weeks visiting his new acquisitions. As usual he was holding his cards very close to his chest. His broad and bare chest.

She did know that he was planning a big

reveal towards the end of the trip—some kind of showdown—and it unnerved her. The anger he felt was completely understandable, but it isolated him, had twisted him into a machine, bent on revenge. Neither of them had done much living over the years, but she had chosen her path out of love and duty. His path was much darker.

But somehow, these last few days, he had seemed lighter. Maybe being back here, confronting some of those demons that haunted him was helping to set him free? The evening they had spent with his aunt had seemed cathartic, but the next day he had decided to leave Rio and head here; she couldn't help wondering if the ghosts in Rio were proving too much.

All she knew was that at some point he was going to have to forgive himself and move on, but his plans for the Caetanos didn't speak of moving on; instead it seemed to root him in the past, and she ached in sympathy when she saw the clouds in his eyes and knew that he was brooding on what might have been.

The rest of the morning passed peacefully. Their room opened straight out onto the beach and Deangelo had retreated to the shady ter-

race to work, waving away her offer to help.
'I know you want to finish that book,' he said.
'Your eyes keep straying towards it.'

'Yes, but I'm here to work,' she protested
half-heartedly, her hands curling around the
book.

'Don't worry, I have plenty for you to do
later, but right now you are free to read. Take
advantage of it.'

'Well, if you insist...'

It was lovely to soak up the sun and read,
but as noon approached and she finally finished the last chapter Harriet began to get
restless. She rolled out of the hammock and
padded over the hot sand. 'Okay,' she said
firmly. 'That's enough.'

He looked up, expression confused, and she
sighed. 'Do you even know where you are?'

'If you were wearing that bikini back in
the office I think HR would have something
to say.'

'You could have been anywhere. You were
completely absorbed. And that's fine, but we
are in near paradise and it seems a shame
for you to sit there and stare at spreadsheets.
You worked all day yesterday; you should
actually spend some time on holiday being
on holiday.'

'You didn't mind when you were reading your book.'

'That is called relaxing. You should try it some time.'

Laughing, he pushed his laptop away. 'So what do you want to do?' His gaze slid to the bedroom, visible through the open doors. 'Take a siesta?'

'At some point, definitely, but what I'd really like to do is take a picnic and go to that little beach those Americans told us about. The one you have to sail to. It sounds idyllic.'

Deangelo didn't move for one moment, his narrowed gaze still focused on his laptop, but then he nodded. 'Okay.'

'Okay? Really?'

'As long as you wear that bikini.'

'It's a deal. Yay! I'll order the picnic and arrange the boat and crew. The Americans said they saw turtles and dolphins. Can you imagine?'

'No crew needed. I'll captain and you can be my crew.'

'It's been a long time since I sailed,' she said doubtfully. The ocean looked pretty flat and peaceful, but it was vaster than she could imagine.

'That's why I'm the captain. Give me an hour and I'll be ready.'

'Perfect!'

As she turned to leave, Harriet put her hand on Deangelo's shoulder and absent-mindedly he reached up to cover it with his own. She paused, looking down at their entwined hands, relishing the feel of his muscle under her palm, of his strong fingers interlaced with hers. It wasn't just that she couldn't have imagined being this free and easy with Deangelo, she couldn't have imagined it with anyone. The longer between dates, the more terrifying the thought of putting herself out there was. Her last relationship had petered out when her boyfriend had told her that she was always tired, that her lack of willingness to do anything was boring, and she couldn't help but agree with him. She had felt dull and boring. If she was him, she would have broken up with her, too. But now she felt full of possibilities. Her life opening up before her. She would always thank Deangelo for that.

The little motorboat was so easy to steer that Harriet had no qualms about taking the helm, enjoying the wind whipping her hair and the spray misting over her bare arms. Once they were a reasonable way out to sea she killed the engine and allowed the boat to bob around for a little, enjoying the sensation of just being on the ocean.

'You know...' Harriet said a little wistfully as she trailed her hand in the cool water. 'When I was little we would always go on holiday to Cornwall. Just the three of us. My sisters didn't come, obviously, they deigned to spend time with us when we went skiing or the year we rented a villa in Tuscany, but Cornwall just wasn't glamorous enough, not the part we went to, anyway. But my mum loved it; she'd holidayed there every year of her life. She'd get more and more excited the nearer we got, as if she were the child. We'd always have a competition over who could see the sea first when we drove there and once there we would spend the whole time kayaking and swimming and surfing. But after she died we couldn't bear to go back. We'd holiday in cities instead, gorge on culture and local food. I didn't know just how much I missed the sea until now.' She inhaled. 'The smell just makes everything seem all right.'

Deangelo reached out to touch her cheek.

'We share that, you and I. We both had that before and after. The old and then the new normal, only the new normal would never measure up.'

'Yes. I suppose we did. It's not just losing a parent, is it? It's the loss of everything else. For me a new home, a new school, a father who seemed to have lost part of him—and then he really did lose part of him. For you…' She paused. For him poverty and loss and a physical reminder of the family who had chosen to cast him out. How could she blame him for the anger that palpably drove him? 'For you, everything. But here we are. We survived, moved on.'

'Yes.' But he didn't sound convinced. Was that because he hadn't actually moved on at all? That part of him was still the bereaved boy wondering what he could have done differently to save his mother?

Maybe she could show him another way. She heard her mother as she ploughed on, telling her she couldn't save everyone, but Harriet ignored the remembered warning, as she had done so many times before. 'Yes, and you know, this trip has shown me that I can't keep putting off working out who I am and what I want to be. Who I want to be. The agency is a start, and it's exciting. But we're all frozen in time somehow, me, Alex, Emilia and Amber. That's partly what drew us together, but I wonder if it gives us permission not to try and move on. Well, no more. I'm going to live and love and dance, even if it hurts me. These last few days, life has been in Technicolor. I want it to stay that way.'

Had she said too much? But wasn't that the point, that she was no longer going to be afraid? It wasn't as if she'd made a big declaration of love, begged him to stay with her. She'd just shown him that she had changed. The question was, had he?

She grinned as he shifted closer. Yes, he had changed—he was wearing shorts for a start, *and* a T-shirt. A comfortable cotton T-shirt with a windsurfer emblazoned on the front. His hair was a tiny bit longer, and a lot more dishevelled than his usual neat crop, and stubble darkened his cheeks and jaw. But most telling of all were the laughter lines creasing his eyes and cheeks. She'd barely seen him crack a smile before. Now he seemed to smile all the time.

Was that because being here was cathartic—or did it possibly have something to do with her?

Placing her hand on his, she leaned closer, inwardly thrilling at her daring, at the way she was emboldened to take the lead, the way he let her, amusement warring with desire in his dark gaze. Her mouth touched his in a kiss, soft and sweet, for a moment, then harder and decadently rich as she relinquished the brief control willingly as his hand slid down her bare back and over her hip. She gasped against his mouth, willing him on, her eyes fluttering shut, only to open again as something behind him snagged her attention. 'Deangelo…' she murmured. 'Look!'

Pulling back just a little, he half turned, only to freeze in place as he saw the same dorsal fin she had seen. *'Golfinho…'* he breathed.

Not daring to move, barely to breathe, Harriet just sat, spellbound, as the dolphin swam lazily past them, submerging momentarily, only to leap in the air, twisting as the sun glinted off its sleek purple-black body. 'It's doing tricks!'

It was almost—almost—close enough to touch, plainly curious about the small bobbing boat and its two inhabitants, swimming away, only to shoot out of the water and twist before swimming back again, treating the pair to an unrivalled display of water gymnastics, clearly enjoying the interaction as much as they were. Harriet was barely aware of Deangelo taking her hand in his, of the way he pulled her close so she sat against him as the dolphin played, the two relaxing enough to laugh out loud at the jumps and games. 'I wish I could swim with him,' Harriet said longingly.

'It's a wild animal, for all it seems so real.'

'I know. And I hate the thought of it being in captivity or tamed in any way. It's perfect wild and free. I feel so privileged it wants to share this time with us.' And as Deangelo dropped a kiss on her head she couldn't help thinking that, although he was the opposite of the dolphin in many ways, constricted by the rules he set himself, imprisoned by the life he chose, she was equally as privileged to share these rare intimate moments with him. Moments to savour, and never to take for granted.

'You know,' Harriet said dreamily, eyes half-closed, 'I take it back. This place *is* paradise. And today was pretty near perfect.'

Deangelo grinned as he ran his hand down her side and felt her gasp. 'Just pretty near?'

'The dolphin was perfect,' she allowed.

'What about what came after the dolphin?' He ran his hand back up, nudging the full underside of her breast, reining in the urge to deepen the touch as she arched ever so slightly.

'You mean the gorgeous beach? And the swimming?'

'The *nude* swimming…' he reminded her, his hand skimming up to her throat and along her jaw. He adored how responsive she was, how uninhibited, how she made him want to worship her completely and unselfishly.

'And the moment we saw the turtle. The dolphin still wins because of the tricks but the turtle comes a really close second in the most-awesome-moment-ever competition.'

'The turtle was amazing,' Deangelo allowed. 'What about after the turtle?'

'The picnic? Yes. That was excellent.'

'Harriet,' he said slowly, drawing one finger down her bare arm, watching the way she shivered under his touch. 'After the picnic…'

'That was excellent, too,' she conceded,

rolling over to meet him. 'Almost perfect, in fact.'

'Only almost?' He retraced the path his finger had taken and her chest rose and fell.

'I'm just saying, practice makes perfect...'

'Is that a challenge, Harriet Fairchild?'

'Are you up to it if it is?'

'Always.' As he said the word the reality of it struck home. That this woman, lying languorously next to him, wanted to be there was nothing short of a miracle. Oh, Deangelo attracted women, most drawn to his money, some by success. A few were intrigued by his brawn and scar, suspecting the rough edges under the tailored suit, but none of them knew him. Harriet did, better than anyone. She knew the ugly truth and she still chose to be here.

Even more miraculously, he wanted her here. He never allowed himself to want anything good or warm or real. Just the coldness of success and revenge. And yet here he was. She made him want to be better, do better. She almost made him forgive himself. 'Always,' he said again, tasting the word as he said it.

He saw Harriet swallow, the flicker of her

eyes. 'Don't worry. I won't hold you to that when we're back.'

'We agreed just one night and yet here we still are,' he reminded her, unsure why he pressed the point. Of course they would go their separate ways when they returned to London. Harriet had a life to lead, a new business and a world to explore. And he? He had no idea what he would do once his revenge had finally been exacted, but one thing hadn't changed—in the end, people always let you down. If he and Harriet tried to extend this understanding, he'd mess it up. That was what he did. Better to not think past today.

'We agreed no strings. So don't think you have to say nice things to make me feel better, because that really isn't necessary.'

'When have you ever known me to do or say anything nice for the sake of it?' Why was he arguing the point when they both knew it would be over? Was it because he wanted to at least pretend that there might be more—or was it because he wanted Harriet to believe it? To know that if he were a different man he would never let her go. That all the clichés were true. She was a for ever kind of woman for one lucky man. And for the first time in for ever he wished that man could be him.

'You do nice things. You always send your girlfriends an expensive necklace when you break up with them.'

'Dates,' he corrected her. 'They are only ever dates. And I have an account at the jewellers and you order and send the necklaces.'

'True. When you put it that way it isn't quite so nice.'

'Soulless even.' He wasn't sure he wanted her to answer that.

'A little,' she conceded. 'But not always. You paid for Beryl's hip replacement.'

'It was interfering with her work and she cleans the office just the way I like it.'

'With a top surgeon and an all-inclusive holiday to recuperate as soon as she could travel.'

'I wanted her back fit and well.'

'You paid for that guy from Accounts to take his kids to Disneyland.'

'Yes.' He could hear the bleakness in his voice. 'They had lost their mum the year before.'

'It was a nice thing to do.'

'Or a way of salving my own guilty conscience? Buying people things doesn't make me nice, Harriet. It's the easiest thing in the world.'

'Choosing the right thing isn't,' she argued. 'That's far trickier. Dad loved Mum and obviously, compared to you, he might not have been rich, but by normal standards he was really well off. But he never quite got her presents right. A flashy convertible when actually she'd have preferred a vintage vehicle. A diamond necklace when she liked Art Deco beads. He never quite got it. But you get it without being told. Look at that library membership you gave me. That was perfect.'

With a sigh Deangelo pulled himself up to sit next to her. 'You always had your nose in a book when you weren't working and the shared house you were living in was tiny. You always said you had no space of your own. I thought you'd like to be able to hide out there at weekends.'

'I did, I do.'

'So there you go. No miracle. Just observation. That's what I do in business. See what needs fixing and find a solution. It's not as complicated as you make it sound.' Deangelo didn't know why he was trying to downplay the gift, nor the time he had spent trying to find her something really special.

He just knew he didn't want her to realise just how much pleasure he had received from giving her something that he knew would make her really happy.

'But that's just it.' Harriet clearly wasn't done, her forehead furrowed as she puzzled out her thoughts. 'I had no idea that was the perfect gift, but somehow you did. It's like the coat. How on earth did you find one to fit me so perfectly?'

'That old coat of yours was no good at all. The colour washed you out; you were always cold in it.'

'How do you know that?'

'Because I know you, Harriet Fairchild. I notice you.'

As soon as he had said the words Deangelo wanted to recall them. Harriet stilled next to him, her eyes the only colour in her suddenly pale face. 'What do you mean?'

'I just told you, I fix problems...'

'No. What do you mean when you say you notice me?'

'You've worked for me for three years. Of course I notice you. If your hip needed replacing then I would have organised that for you too.'

'That's good to know,' she said drily. 'But

Deangelo. Those gifts. The membership, the coat. Those ballet tickets—how did you know my mother took me to see *The Nutcracker* every Christmas?'

'Doesn't everyone's mother take them to see *The Nutcracker* every Christmas?'

'No. They don't. They're the most perfect things I ever received. And they're not practical. They don't solve any problems...'

'Nonsense. That old coat could have made you ill.'

'The library?'

'Everyone needs space of their own, Harriet. I spent my teenage years sharing a small house with ten relatives. I know this.'

'The tickets?'

'You deserve to be happy.' Once again words he had no idea he was going to say echoed around the room as once again Harriet froze, as if processing them.

'You were an excellent PA; you made my life run smoothly. You deserved a reward.' He could hear the chilling tone in his voice, feel the walls closing back in as he said the cold words.

'That's all it was?'

'That's all it was. I told you I'm not nice.' Her next words were so soft he could barely hear them. 'I know that makes sense. That's what I believed. I mean, nothing else makes any sense. But you know what else makes no sense? Insisting I accompany you on this trip. You need barely any support. Any decent temp could have done it. Any reasonable actress could have pretended to be your wife.'

'I needed someone I could trust.'

'And another thing. Why are you working so hard to push me away? Trying to prove how not nice you are when every gesture tells me something different—when you notice me? When you tell me *always*?'

It was his turn to freeze. For he had said that word not once but twice. He'd told her he'd noticed her. Let his guard down. Why? Because he wanted her to look in the mirror and see what he saw in her. To stop putting herself down and behind, to believe.

He was a man who had everything and possessed nothing. Who made billions from the intangible, using algorithms to profit from other people's work and ingenuity. A man who lived alone, who let no one close. A man frightened of letting anyone in, who deserved nothing. Who didn't trust himself not to let people down. Even now, he was proving himself no better than his father, the man who'd seduced his housekeeper and left her with nothing. He had sworn never to be like the Caetanos and yet here he was, with his PA in his bed.

He knew it was wrong—and yet it felt so right. He also knew he couldn't dent her new-found self-confidence, that to do so would be a crime greater than any his father had committed.

He knew he had to be honest. And that was the most terrifying thing of all.

'I needed you with me on this trip because I couldn't imagine anyone else by my side when I returned to Rio.' He couldn't look at her as he spoke. 'I needed you to play my bride because I couldn't imagine making it seem genuine with anyone else.' She gave a sharp intake of breath but said nothing. 'I bought you the coat because I saw it and knew you would look beautiful in it. I bought you the ballet tickets because I hear you when you talk to me, even when I don't acknowledge it, and one day you mentioned it was opening night and it always made you think of your mother.'

Still she said nothing but she crept a little closer, closing the gap that had opened up between them, and laid her head on his shoulder, her hand finding his and clutching it.

Now he had started he wasn't sure he could stop. 'I liked the way you smiled and said good morning as if you meant it, not because it was a courtesy. I saw you counsel your friends, and heard you speak to your father on the phone three times a day, always patient, even when I could see frustrated tears in your eyes. I saw how you would get lost in a book, even the longest flight an opportunity to read, not a chore, but you always put work first. I saw the way you asked nothing from anyone but gave—and I thought it was time you got put first. I wanted to see you smile. You have a beautiful smile.'

He stopped. There were more words, more feelings, locked up inside but he had no idea how to reach them, if he even dared to try. Harriet lifted her head from his shoulder and turned to him, her eyes damp with tears. 'Thank you. Thank you for saying that.'

'It's true, Harriet. Like I told you, I'm not nice.'

He tilted her chin so that he could look straight into her eyes, imprint his words on her. 'I didn't want you to leave. But it's right you start to live. That you build your family and figure out who you are and where you want to be. I admire that. Respect it.'

'I wish you the same,' she whispered, covering his hand with hers, tilting her chin higher so her mouth brushed his once and then again. 'You need to learn to live as well. To build. Life's far too short to spend it locked away, Deangelo.'

He deepened the kiss, laying her back on the bed, covering her body with his. Deangelo wished that he could believe her words. But some people were safer locked away and times like this nothing but a brief parole. But as her hands travelled down his back, pulling him closer, he allowed himself the indulgence of one wish. That he could be different, that his scars could be external only, that he could be allowed happiness with a woman like this.

CHAPTER ELEVEN

HARRIET STRETCHED SLEEPILY, not wanting to open her eyes quite yet, wanting to stay in this quiet, contented moment for ever. Last night's lovemaking had been like nothing she had ever experienced. Tender, sweet. Loving.

She stilled. Loving?

That wasn't in their agreement, not the formal or the informal.

And yet…

Somehow, over the last week, she had told Deangelo more about herself than any other person, including her friends and her father. And she suspected the same was equally true of him. Was it because they trusted each other, because they had worked together for so long, so intensely, that there were few barriers? She had seen Deangelo tired and frustrated, elated, working tirelessly to solve puzzles. And he? He had noticed her—all those days and weeks and months when she'd thought he saw her as nothing but some kind of competent office robot he had seen straight into the soul of her.

They trusted each other. And this was the last time they would work together. He would return to his South Bank tower and she to her Chelsea townhouse and it was unlikely their paths would ever cross again. This trip would be a cherished memory for her to examine on those long, dark nights of the soul that seemed to occur far too often. Or better, she could use it as a catalyst to move her life forward in a direction she chose.

She'd been bold and playful and seductive. She'd been open to new experiences. She'd seen this trip as an adventure and grabbed it with both hands. Surely she could repeat that once back in London?

Rolling over, she opened her eyes and allowed herself the luxury of watching Deangelo with no barriers between them. It was rare for him to sleep and her to be awake and she luxuriated in it, starting at the top of the dark head, her gaze moving slowly down the unusually peaceful face, his mouth relaxed in sleep giving him a relaxed air seldom seen in waking hours. She paused as she reached the scar, the visible reminder of his banishment from the family who spurned him, the never-fading reminder of the day he had swallowed his pride to help his mother and failed. That day had changed him, hardened him, driven him. Was he capable of letting go and moving on? She hoped so. Further down, the sensuous mouth and firm chin, broad shoulders and chest, ridged with muscle and yet capable of utter gentleness. Dark silky hair running down to the kind of abs not usually found on deskbound businessmen, then down again…

'Like what you see?'

Damn. How did he do that? Wake so instantly and alertly. Embarrassed heat flushed through her, although she tried to hide it, meeting his amused gaze full-on. 'It's not bad.'

How she had the *sangfroid* to tease him like that, to lie here, only half-covered by her sheet, utterly comfortable in such intimacy she didn't know. But she had no fear, no worries about her inadequacies, no desire to cover her stretch marks or overly ample curves. From being a skinny child, her hips and breasts had grown in adolescence, giving her an hourglass figure she had no idea how to live in, her height another torment for a girl who just wanted to hide in a reading nook somewhere. With no mother to reassure her, a father who thought of her as a little girl and slender toned half-sisters who looked her up and down—and side to side—with barely hidden scorn, Harriet had spent half her life dressing to hide and shroud. But no more. Deangelo had made her body feel like something that deserved worshipping—and worship it he had. The heat intensified and this time she made no move to hide it, smiling across at him instead.

'That's not what you said last night,' he said, returning her smile with an intimate one of his own, part wolf but with a hint of sweetness that made her chest ache and stomach twist. With lust, yes, with need and want, but with something more.

And she wasn't sure she wanted to face that something more.

'So, what do you want to do today?' she asked, aware she was retreating but unable to do anything about it. 'I thought we might walk into the village and take a look. If you did decide to turn this place from an all-inclusive fortress where guests live in a protected bubble to somewhere that feeds into and helps the local economy it would be a good idea to see what the village actually offers.'

Deangelo's smile disappeared, his expression guarded once more, as if the sweet intimacy had never been. 'You're probably right. But I haven't decided what to do yet.'

'To do about what?'

'About this place, about any of them. This isn't just about gaining control of my father's business, Harriet. It's about justice. I could turn the hotels around, sure, invest in them. But how does that help achieve justice? The Caetanos will reap the rewards without lifting a finger. I want them to lose everything. To know what it is like to see everything they think they are stripped away from them.'

Harriet sat up, chilled despite the heat of the day. 'But how on earth will you do that?'

He shrugged. 'Maybe sell the hotels for nothing. Or let them continue to run them into the ground. I haven't decided yet.'

'Or you could put every penny of profit back into the hotels and make a success of them, despite their mismanagement. Thousands of people work for these hotels; you can't endanger their jobs because of a personal vendetta.' She couldn't quite believe what she was hearing. How could the man who put so much effort into transforming lives be so casual about the people who worked for the Caetanos? 'If not then yes, sell them to someone who will invest and build; don't allow them to wither just to prove a point.'

His expression hardened. 'I would make sure the employees were compensated.'

'Even so...' She lay back down, unease still twisting through her. This wasn't right. 'Compensation doesn't make up for the lack of a livelihood, or purpose.'

'You said yourself this place does nothing for the local economy. No one who comes here enhances the local area at all.'

'No, but they could. And you could drive that.'

'I'm not a hotelier.'

'You own a hotel in Rio, run it as a social enterprise. You could do exactly the same here. Rename them, invest every penny of profit in them and don't hand anything to the Caetanos. You'll achieve the same end but do a lot of good along the way. But, better still, pay them off. Buy the rest of the chain and then walk away, severing all links. Act fair. Show them they are nothing. That's got to be the better win.'

But he had completely shut down. 'I've worked for this for over ten years, Harriet. Everything I have done has been to this end. And you want me to pay them off for their trouble and let them walk away scot-free?'

'I want you to move on.' Suddenly uncomfortable with her state of undress, Harriet slid out of the bed and grabbed the light silk robe she'd bought last week. To play a part, true, but it shocked her how quickly she had slid into accepting the situation, wearing the expensive clothes and accessories as easily as if she had paid for them herself. How quickly her fourth finger had grown used to the rings and how she looked for the flash of blue when the sapphire caught the light. 'You are letting what happened define you.'

'It shaped me,' he said tightly, following her out of the bed and disappearing into the en suite bathroom, closing the door firmly behind him. Harriet's stomach dropped, the feeling of ease and rightness she'd woken up with dropping with it. She should have kept quiet. This was none of her business.

But how could she? Deangelo had always encouraged her to state her opinion, always listened courteously. But that was when their relationship was professional, not personal. When her opinion was purely business-related, not the very heart of him.

Besides, it wasn't as if she didn't know he was ruthless; no one could be as successful as he was without a streak of coldness.

Harriet made sure the robe was firmly tied, slipped on a pair of flip-flops and headed out to the terrace, where she knew their breakfast had been left. Sure enough, a steaming coffee pot sat on the wide wooden table, along with a jug of covered fruit juice and lidded platters which, she knew from experience, contained tiny tasty pastries, slices of fresh fruit and yogurt. But she wasn't at all hungry, unable to stomach anything else but the bitter Brazilian coffee. Pouring a cup, she wandered along the terrace to where her hammock lay, swaying ever so slightly in the faint breeze. Yesterday she had been so happy.

Today reality was beginning to reassert itself and it wasn't a comfortable process.

No matter how tender Deangelo might be, no matter how much they might play the honeymooning couple, nothing had actually changed. Their worlds were miles and miles apart. Not just because of money or position, but because of what they wanted. Harriet wanted a family, not just the friends she had made over the last few years, but a husband and children. She'd just been too scared to articulate that need to herself. To dare to think beyond the next day. She knew all too well what it felt like to lose everything, both instantly and also so slowly that the unthinkable began to be normal.

This last week had shown her just what loving and being loved could be like. Not that Deangelo loved her, she knew that, nor she him…

She placed her coffee cup down, hands shaking, spilling the dark, thick liquid onto the table. Love? Where had thought come from? So she had admitted that she found Deangelo sexy. That she desired him. That maybe, if she was really honest with herself, she had secretly felt that way for a long time. Had been proud of the close relationship they'd shared, that she so often received one of his rare smiles, that he liked her to accompany him wherever he went, whether business trips abroad or the rare occasion he accepted a corporate invitation. That she liked entering rooms by his side, even if her demure shapeless dresses and the tablet she carried rather than a bag made it clear her position. She liked it when he asked her opinion, when he listened.

People thought of him as a soulless, joyless automaton and she would agree. But she'd always known he was more. She'd just been scared to admit it. To admit how much she noticed him.

As he had noticed her. Maybe that was it. Just occasionally he made her feel special and that was so rare in her life she absorbed those moments, holding them close, needing them. But was that love? How could it be? It was all about her, about how she felt. Love wasn't selfish. It shouldn't be.

How could she love the man who tried to change the system that had nearly broken him? The man who quietly made things better, never asking for praise or recognition? The man who danced like the devil and made love like an angel?

How could she not? Because it was hopeless? Because he was so broken there was no way of fixing him? Because he didn't love her, didn't love anyone? If only love worked that way.

Oh, God. She had fallen in love with him. What an utter idiot she was.

Mechanically, she grasped for her bag, realising it was still in the room. She needed her phone, to read HEAA emails and absorb herself in something she had some control over. Rising to her feet, she walked the few yards slowly, still unable to process what had just happened, what she had admitted to herself and what it meant.

The shutter doors were pulled to and she pushed them open, halting at the sight of Deangelo standing in the middle of the large room, a towel looped round his hips, hair wet and slicked back. It was a sumptuous space, a one-room villa dominated by the wooden four-poster, decked in gauzy white curtains. A white sofa and matching chairs were placed on the opposite side of the room, a dining table and chairs behind them. At the back, doors led to his and hers bathrooms. Huge shuttered windows could be un-shuttered to let the outside in, with beach and sea views on three of the four sides. It was the most glorious place Harriet had ever seen.

But, next to him, it was nothing. He dominated the space, not just with his physical size, but with his aura. How could she not love him? But saving him was a whole different matter and one that might just be beyond her.

Harriet didn't speak, just stood by the door staring at him, the morning sunshine framing her, highlighting her strawberry-blonde hair to a golden glow, shining off her lightly tanned skin. She looked like an angel. An angel come to deliver him or to deliver judgement on him. Deangelo wasn't sure which he wanted; he knew which one he deserved.

But hadn't she already begun the process? Taken his certainty and shaken it. He'd come here for revenge, but now he no longer knew if that was the right path.

And after so many years pursuing that path, uncertainty was as unwelcome as it was disconcerting. He had vowed to avenge his mother. How could he turn away now when he was so close?

But Harriet's words rung true, chiming in with the conscience he had been doing his best to ignore. His actions didn't just affect himself. If he was too ruthless, then he was no better than the family who had disowned him, not caring who he trampled in the process, how many lives he destroyed.

'I just wanted to get my bag,' she said, stepping tentatively into the room as if she were afraid of him, afraid of who he really was deep down. As if she could see the unworthiness deep in his soul, even after all they had shared, and at that moment Deangelo knew with cool clarity that the honeymoon was over.

'Of course.'

'I was thinking…'

But he cut in first. She didn't need to say anything.

'I need to get back to the city.'

'Right. Okay. That's…'

'It's time to end this.'

Disappointment clouded her expression for a moment before the polite, bland expression of old reappeared. 'You're the boss.'

Deangelo curled his hands into fists, holding back the words trying to burst out of him. *Try to understand—this is all I have, all I am. Can't you love me anyway? Find me worthy, despite my monstrousness.*

Love? Where had that come from? Love was weakness. If you didn't love then you couldn't lose. If you weren't loved then you couldn't fail someone. He'd spent his whole adult life making sure he never got close enough to anyone for any kind of love, keeping even his mother's family at arm's length, even the aunt who had given him a home, the aunt who had fought tirelessly to get him a scholarship to a good school, to get the education which had led to Cambridge and a new life. Materially she wanted for nothing, although she had elected to stay and work in the *favela*, throwing that same spirit which had propelled Deangelo to school into community projects. But this trip was the first time he had visited her since he had left. She deserved better, but he didn't know how to give her more.

Harriet deserved better. He suspected she knew that. Because she might be able to save him but he was much more likely to drag her down.

'Pack your things. I'll get Reception to order a car...'

'I'll do that,' she said quickly. 'My job, remember? Do you want to head back to Rio? Not the same hotel?'

'Good God, no.' But his reaction wasn't because of the faded glory or the location; it was because he didn't want to return to the suite where he had first made love to Harriet, where they had shared a hot, sweet, fevered night, one that was supposed to be a one and only. If it had been, would the inevitable parting be easier?

'No, I thought not. I'll find us somewhere more suitable. How long do you want to stay in Rio? Or would you like to stay somewhere else until the shareholders' meeting? One of the other hotels maybe, to get a different perspective?'

Deangelo had been born in Rio and stayed there until the day he had flown to England. He'd been born in a vast country full of natural wonders, full of incredible wildlife, and he had never seen more than a few square miles. But what was the point of visiting hotels he had no interest in running, in places he would never return to? His life was over the ocean now.

'We'll stay in Rio for the rest of the allotted time. It'll take time to put the right compensation packages for workers together, to decide what to do with the hotels.'

'You've made your mind up then?'

'Harriet, it never changed.'

She nodded, a dignified acknowledgement—or capitulation—and his heart cracked, knowing he had just pushed away the one person who might have saved him.

'Fine. I'll get dressed and then book the car and the hotel.' She walked, straight-backed, past him and into her bathroom, the door shutting firmly behind her. Deangelo stood watching the door for a few seconds, wondering what would happen if he was brave enough to tap on it, to ask her to help him be someone new, to help him move on. But as he moved he caught sight of his reflection, the faded scar reminding him of a duty as ingrained as destiny and, turning, he scooped up his laptop and headed out to the terrace and coffee to work.

But as he walked out Harriet's words from the other day returned to him. Was this what his mother would have wanted? She had been fiery, yes. Passionate. Quick to anger, quicker to laugh. And she had loved him. Wholeheartedly. The only person who ever had. Would she have wanted him to lock himself away? If she was looking down, was she proud of all he had achieved—or grieving who he had become?

How could he answer that? All he knew

was that revenge had driven him all these years and he had no idea how to stop.

He'd always been able to lose himself in work and today was no exception. Opening his laptop allowed him back into a safe world where all he had to lose was money. He opened a report on potential investments and concentrated on projections and strategies, ruthlessly shutting out the birdsong, the sigh of the waves, the view. This was his life, the rest just a distraction. And if his chest felt hollow and his throat ached, well, he'd just drink some more coffee and carry on. It was all he knew how to do.

The report was absorbing enough to allow him to slip back into his safe space until a cry brought him back to awareness of his surroundings, the sun hot on his back a reminder he wasn't at his desk. Another strangled sob brought him to his feet and back into the bedroom before he was even aware what he was doing, pulse hammering.

'What's wrong? Are you hurt?'

Harriet was sitting on the bed, her phone in her hand, face white, eyes wide in shock. 'I…'

'What's happened?'

'It's my dad. He's had a stroke. The home

just called. They said I need to get back straight away. Oh, Deangelo. I think he's dying. I'm going to be all alone. What will I do?'

The next couple of hours passed in a blur, Deangelo ruthlessly taking control, sending Harriet to pack while he organised a car to take her straight to the airport where his pilot would be waiting for her. After her bags were packed she made call after call, to her friends, to the hospital and, fruitlessly it seemed, tried to track down her sisters.

She was making another attempt to find her sisters when Reception alerted Deangelo that the car had arrived and that a porter would be there to collect Harriet's bags in the next few minutes. Deangelo walked back into the room. It looked bare and lonely with Harriet's possessions missing, the suitcases by the door poignant. If he was the kind of man to indulge in poignancy, that was.

Walking over to the sofa where she sat hunched, phone clamped to her ear, Deangelo laid one hand gently on her shoulder. 'It's time,' he said.

Harriet only nodded as she laid the phone in her lap. She sat very still, as if gathering her strength, then rose stiffly to her feet. As she did so the porter rapped gently on the door and, after a quick consultation with Deangelo, took her bags.

'The car will take you straight to the airport. Tony is waiting there for you and will fly you straight back to London, where another car will meet you.'

'Fine. Thanks. Oh, my clothes? My own clothes?'

'Already on board.'

'Great. I'll have these returned to you after…once I'm home.'

'Keep them; they look better on you.' But the feeble joke didn't raise even a glimmer of a smile.

'I can't. It doesn't seem right.'

'Consider them a bonus,' he said, more bitterly than he intended, but she didn't respond. He'd seen Harriet worried before, upset before, but never this bleak. Hopeless, hands twisting as she stood there.

'Oh!' She stilled her hands, staring down at them. 'The rings.'

'They were made for you. Keep them.' He'd ordered them weeks ago, designed

them just for her, the entwined branches and leaves symbolising her strength and ability to renew and carry on, the sapphire matching her eyes.

'They are the most beautiful rings I have ever seen. But I can't keep them, Deangelo.' As she spoke she slid them off her finger and laid them in his palm, closing his hand over the delicate circles. 'Right.'

'I'll walk you to the car.'

'No. Please. I can manage.' She touched his cheek, the scarred cheek, with one gentle caress then walked to the door, stopping just before she stepped outside and turned, eyes bright with unshed tears. 'I'm frightened, Deangelo. My father is all I have. Without him I am truly alone. I don't know if I can do this by myself.'

'Hey,' he said roughly, trying to push the emotion away, to stay strong. 'If anyone can handle this, you can.'

'Why do people always leave me?' she whispered, and his heart twisted.

'Harriet, you and I know that the only people we can rely on are ourselves. It's not easy, but that's the way it is. At least we don't get let down this way.'

'If that's true, why did you need me for this trip?'

It was his turn to freeze. 'I knew you'd get the job done. I trusted you.'

'I can't be the only person you trust.'

'It was a business decision, pure and simple.'

But was it, or had it been simply that he couldn't have faced coming home without her? No. That wasn't how he operated; it couldn't be. It would make him weak, vulnerable, to need someone else in that way.

'Come with me,' she said, and his chest thumped painfully at the hope in her voice, in her expression. 'Walk away from revenge and anger. I don't want to do this alone, Deangelo. I want to do this with you. With someone who knows me, who notices me, with someone I trust…' She took a deep breath. 'With someone I love.'

The pain in his chest intensified, the roar of his blood competing with the thud of his heart. For one moment he considered agreeing, leaving Brazil, the Caetanos, his revenge behind, flying back with her, supporting her the way she needed him to. The way she hadn't been afraid to ask him to. He envied her courage. 'Don't waste your love on me, Harriet. I'm not worth it.'

She nodded, one tear falling as she tried to smile. 'That's not how love works, Deangelo. I hope your revenge is worth it.' And then she turned and was gone, leaving him alone once again. Just as he was meant to be.

Only it hadn't hurt this way for a very long time.

CHAPTER TWELVE

'HERE—EAT THIS.'

Deangelo's aunt placed a plate of warm, spicy cookies in front of him, adding a glass of milk, as if he were still the skinny, lost ten-year-old who had come to live with her. Her house was bigger now, thanks to him, but it had the same feel as the old overcrowded cottage clinging to the hillside, her eclectic taste marrying vintage with modern, brightly coloured pictures and ornaments jostling for prominence, the walls and shelves covered with photos of her children and grandchildren. In the centre of the bookshelf was a photo of Deangelo and his mother, a formal one taken when they still lived on the estate. She followed Deangelo's gaze and her face softened.

'She looked so happy. She was so happy. She loved him, your father, never doubt that.'

'But did he love her?'

'I believe so. She believed so. She would never have stayed if she didn't. And she never blamed him for how things turned out. Whether he made a will and it was suppressed, or he forgot to write one we'll never know. But she was never bitter. It was the way things were.'

'She would never have died if she hadn't lost everything.'

'We don't know that. All we can do is live with how things are. Find happiness in what we have. Have you heard from Harriet?'

The last question was shot straight at him. His aunt had taken to Harriet and was sad to hear of her troubles. 'No. I don't want to bother her when she has so much to worry about.'

'Nonsense—why would you be bothering her? She'll want to know you're thinking of her.'

'We're not together, not like that. She worked for me, that's all.' The lies were bitter on his tongue and he wasn't surprised when his aunt laughed.

'You tell yourself that, but I know when two people are mad about each other. I was the eldest of five and I had eight children of my own. You think I haven't seen couples fall in love over and over again? The only thing I don't understand is why you are still here and not back in England, helping her. You know how hard it is to lose your only parent.'

'She lost her father long ago in some ways.' But he knew, despite the illness and the toll it had taken on her whole life, it would devastate Harriet if her father died. 'What did you mean, mad about each other?' His heart thumped as he asked the question. His aunt probably saw what she expected to see in a young couple. But curiosity won out all the same.

She shrugged. 'It's the way you moved, like you were dancing, always in time. The way you would watch each other, almost surreptitiously, checking you were both okay. Little smiles, little touches, moments when it was as if you were alone in the universe. There's a rhythm with a couple in tune, and you two had it. So why did you let her go alone? Your mother would be very disappointed in you.'

'I let everyone down, Tia Luisa.' As he said the words he saw the sorrow in Harriet's eyes as she had asked him to come with her—and the sorrow when she'd told him she loved him. She'd known it was hopeless, that he was hopeless, but she'd tried anyway. 'She's better off without me in her life.' She'd get over him soon enough. Find someone who loved her the way she deserved. His hands curled into fists at the thought but he relished the pain. He deserved it.

'You're letting her down right now. By doing nothing.' Her voice softened as she sat next to him, one warm hand on his arm. 'You have all the money anyone could want, Deangelo, but if you are too afraid to love then what good is it? Your mother would want you to live, to dare to love, to take that risk. Of course there are no guarantees; humans are built that way. But that's the adventure. Your mother risked it all for your father.'

'And she lost.'

'She didn't lose. She had twelve happy years and she had you. She wouldn't have changed any of that for anything. Believe me.'

'I let her down. I was so angry with her when we came here, acted so badly, couldn't get her the money she needed...'

'All she wanted from you was for you to be happy. To be the good, honourable man she knew you could be. Maybe Harriet will make you happy, maybe not, but if you don't try, and keep trying, then you dishonour your mother. But you can never dishonour her by love.'

'I promised I would get my revenge, that I would wipe the Caetanos out of society.' He was pleading for his aunt to understand, to sanction his actions.

'Your father was a Caetano. She would want you to preserve his legacy and show his children the mercy they didn't show you. It's your decision, Deangelo, and I will stand by you whatever you decide. That's what families do. But tonight I will pray that you choose love. It's what your mother would want for you. It's what you should want for yourself.'

She squeezed his arm before heading out of the kitchen, leaving him alone with the milk and cookies and wondering if his mother wouldn't want him to pursue vengeance then who was all this really for?

And, more importantly, wondering if Harriet was coping, or if she still had that lost, scared expression in her eyes. His aunt was right—she needed him. Maybe she loved him, maybe not, but he loved her and she needed him. He was doing no good, skulking here, like Achilles withdrawing from battle, revenge no longer the driving force it had once been. If he let Harriet face her father's illness alone then he didn't deserve any happiness. It was time to let go of his hate and his fear. It was time to hope.

'Can I get you anything?' Amber asked, her voice hushed, as it had been since Harriet returned home a week ago.

Harriet shook her head. 'No. But thank you.'

'You haven't eaten anything.'

'I know. I don't mean to be ungrateful; you have worked so hard...'

But her friend waved the comment away. 'When I'm stressed I bake; you know that. I don't know what else to do.'

'It's appreciated, it really is. I just can't seem to get hungry somehow.'

'Don't worry.' Emilia came into the little sitting/dining room they used at the back of the house. 'The rest of us are eating like kings. Or queens. That broccoli quiche was especially good, Amber. Feel free to stress-bake that again. How's your dad doing today, Harriet?'

The churning in her stomach intensified. 'The same. He just hates being in the hospital so much. He has no idea why he's there and why he can't get out of bed. The sooner he gets back to the home the better.'

'Have your sisters been to visit again?'

'No.' Harriet grimaced. 'I'm such a fool. When I saw them I actually thought things might change, that they'd want to be involved, especially when I reassured them that I wouldn't be asking for money any more. But their faces… They were disgusted by him, by their own father. All those years I thought that one day we might be a family again. But now I don't think I can forgive them for their rejection of Dad, even if I can for the way they treated me.'

Amber squeezed her hand sympathetically before retreating to the kitchen, murmuring something about Bundt cakes and a new recipe she wanted to try out. Emilia hovered for a moment, her expressive eyes dark with sorrow. 'Don't let it define you, Harriet. Families are complicated beasts; that's why I am eternally grateful we have each other.'

'Me too,' Harriet reassured her. 'You and Amber and Alexandra are the sisters I chose, and I know how lucky that makes me.' But the anger she felt towards her actual sisters shocked her in its righteousness and heat. She'd spent so long wanting their approval and acceptance, to be part of their closeness, dreaming of weekend barbecues and long Sunday lunches; now she didn't care if she never saw them again. Was this how Deangelo felt? Had he always wanted his older, legitimate siblings to accept him; had their actions not just scarred him physically but emotionally as well? Did his desire for revenge stem from more than his loss of his home, from more even than his mother's death, but from not being thought good enough to be part of their family? Harriet knew how that felt. She'd always known, but she had still hoped.

Without that hope her feelings were dark and murky. It was easy to see how they could harden and warp. She had friends who loved her to steer and guide her, to remind her of what love and real family bonds were, to pull her back into the light. Who had helped Deangelo? His aunt had done her best, with eight children of her own and an uncertain income she had managed to keep him clothed and fed, sorted his education, but would she have had the time to see the hate festering behind his grief?

Probably not. Deangelo needed understanding and patience, just like she did. Was it too late? For him? For them?

At that moment Amber returned bearing a tray heaped with a teapot and cups, cake and scones and sat it down on the table in front of Harriet. 'House meeting,' she announced.

By the time the tea had been poured and cakes and scones distributed, Alexandra had arrived back and joined them. Looking around at her friends, Harriet felt a twinge of optimism. None of them had had it easy the last few years, yet here they were, planning for the future with hope. Buoyed by the thought, she managed a couple of mouthfuls of scone and a bite of cake, to Amber's beaming approval.

'So,' Emilia said, pushing her plate away. 'Do you want to talk about it?'

'No.' Harriet smiled gratefully at her friends. 'You've all done more than enough, covering my work, coming to the hospital with me, unpacking my bags, even...'

'She doesn't mean talk about your father, although obviously we're here if you need to,' Alexandra added quickly. 'But Em means do you want to talk about your trip to Brazil?'

'You've been withdrawn since you got back, beyond your worry about your father. After all, he was out of danger by the time you landed. I know that's still stressful, but your loss of appetite, the way you keep drifting off into a daydream, the fact you're not sleeping. It's a small house.' Emilia smiled at her apologetically. 'We just want to know you're okay. It's not that we've been discussing you behind your back; it's more that we're all worried and realised that we're worried about the same thing.'

'I'm fine.' But her voice squeaked on the words, the lump in her throat preventing her from saying anything more.

'Harriet, sweetie, did something happen between you and Deangelo?'

'Define "something."'

'I knew it!' Amber said.

'Oh, Harriet. Are you okay? Do you need us to go over there with lighted pitchforks and tear his castle down? Because we will.' Alexandra could be downright scary when she wanted to be.

'No. No, not at all. I am fine. At least, I will be.'

'You fell in love with him,' Emilia said.

'She was always in love with him.' Alexandra reached over and covered Harriet's hand. 'She's just realised it, that's all.'

'Does he love you back?'

How Harriet wished she could answer the hope in Amber's eyes with something positive. 'No,' she said instead. 'At least, he could be. I think he has feelings for me. I know he notices me. But he doesn't know how to love. He's scared to. And I get that. I feel the same way.'

'You deserve more,' Emilia said fiercely.

'I do. But so does he. I just wish I knew how to reach him. I tried. I really tried, Em.'

'Then he's a fool, for all his billions.'

'Maybe.' But as Harriet tried to show her friends how okay she really was she couldn't help but see him as she had walked away— tall, proud, indomitable and so alone it had broken her heart.

As his aunt had predicted, revenge wasn't all it was cracked up to be. Even the big reveal had lacked the piquancy Deangelo had hoped for. Oh, his brothers had blustered and sworn, his sister paled before pleading for her children's share to be preserved if nothing else. But there had been no sense of righteousness. No flaming sword. No resolution. All Deangelo had been able to see was the disappointment in Harriet's face as she had walked away, the hope when she had asked him to come with her. How brave and full of courage she was to have told him she loved him. Harriet, who knew his secrets. Harriet, who knew his fears. Harriet, who feared rejection and hurt and loneliness, had risked all three to try and reach him. And he had failed her, just as he had failed his mother.

For what? For a sense of flatness as he sat opposite the Caetanos and considered devastating their lives as they had devastated his.

Only in the end he hadn't. Because he hadn't been able to go through with it. Oh, he was still the majority shareholder, but the Caetano hotels were still trading. They'd be managed from within Aion, true; his siblings would no longer be able to cream off profits or sell their shares, unless to him, and they wouldn't be penniless, although they would be living on reduced dividends while the hotels were restored to health. He'd even suggested that any nephews or nieces who wanted to be involved could work at Aion.

Why? It wasn't as if the gestures had softened his siblings' attitude to him, or made them feel any more familial towards him. But then he hadn't done it for them. He'd done it for Harriet.

He'd done it for his mother. She would never have wanted him to have followed the dark lonely path he had been on for so long, her death the catalyst. He had dishonoured her memory, dishonoured his upbringing, dishonoured himself.

Worse, he had been a fool, let the best chance he had at redemption walk out of his life without a backward glance, let her go alone to face a difficult situation, and the relief her father's stroke hadn't been as bad as first feared in no way negated that.

It had been a long week. The longest, the hardest, the darkest since his mother's death. A week of looking into the darkest depths of his soul and not liking what he saw there. Not some kind of wounded superhero but more a villain, lurking rather than living, contributing nothing except from afar, too scared of rejection from those he respected to reach out.

No more. He needed to start living in the world, not aside from it.

And if it was too late for Harriet—no, he couldn't think that, not just yet.

Deangelo looked out of the window at the darkness. Usually he loved these moments, alone on his plane, the biggest symbol of success there could be, returning to the city he had conquered. But today he was acutely aware of an ache in his chest. Homesickness. A yearning for the dirty, noisy, chaotic streets of Rio and the people who lived there.

But Harriet was in London. So that was where he needed to be.

It was morning when he landed and as usual he bypassed all the usual tedious airport procedures, money and status ensuring he could leave the airport quickly and discreetly. A marked contrast to that very first flight when, cramped from the long journey he had endured in Economy, he had queued for hours to have his visa scrutinised by hostile border agents.

Today he walked to where his car and driver were waiting for him on the airfield, his dual nationality making border controls a quick, respectful formality. Normality resumed.

Except nothing was the same.

He'd sent his instructions from the plane.

He was to be driven to Chelsea, after a quick stop across the river in Vauxhall, where Deangelo had arranged for a seller at the famous flower market to stay open especially for him. As the car drove away from New Covent Garden's gates and headed across the bridge he was conscious of a new feeling. Nerves. He couldn't remember the last time he had felt nervous. But then again he couldn't remember the last time he'd had something to win. Or to lose.

The streets narrowed as the driver began to make his way through the well-heeled back streets of Chelsea, the bohemian-looking painted and Georgian houses hiding multi-million-pound makeovers and absentee owners. With a jolt Deangelo realised he didn't want to live alone in his tower any more, nor did he want to live somewhere like this, surrounded by other obscenely rich types; he wanted to be back in a community. Be part of something, contribute to it. No more shutting himself away.

His nerves intensified as the driver turned into the quiet Georgian streets and pulled up outside the freshly painted grey front door of the Happy Ever After Agency. Pots filled with lush green plants stood sentry either side of the entrance. Deangelo stood squarely between them and rang the bell. He didn't have too long to wait before a tall, elegant woman opened the door. She stood there for a moment, shock mingling with worry on her austerely beautiful face.

'Yes?' she said at last.

'Hello…' Deangelo searched his memory. This was the PR girl, wasn't it? Alexandra? He risked it. 'Hello, Alexandra. Is Harriet here?'

'I'll see if she wants to be.' And the door closed in his face. Deangelo blinked. It was a long time since he'd been left out on the door-step. He set his jaw and waited, shifting as the seconds turned into minutes, acutely aware of his driver, waiting and witnessing this new and much-needed exercise in humility.

After a few minutes the door opened again, a different woman standing there, an identical shocked and worried expression on her face. 'She'll see you. But I need to tell you, she's had a hard week. If you're here to upset her…'

'I'm not,' he interrupted her and she regarded him unsmilingly before nodding.

'Come in then. We're all at home, within calling distance.' The last words were clearly a threat and a promise and Deangelo couldn't help recalling Harriet's words about building her own family.

'She's lucky to have you.'

A surprised smile softened her pretty but solemn face. 'We're lucky to have her. But I suspect you know that, don't you?'

A few strides and he was through the house and back in the sitting/dining conservatory where he had first persuaded Harriet to come and work for him again. Because he needed her in Rio, or because he needed her? He didn't trust his own motivations back then, not now. He suspected he'd loved her for far longer than he knew. All he knew was once he'd realised she was gone he'd have done anything to get her back.

That hadn't changed.

The conservatory door was open onto the large courtyard garden beyond. Looking back, he saw the three other occupants of the house standing grouped in the kitchen, just beyond hearing distance but watching. The smallest—Amber—nodded encouragingly and Deangelo stepped out of the door and into the courtyard. More flower-filled pots ringed the whitewashed walls, a wrought-iron bench set at one end. Harriet sat on the bench, a book in her hands, but for once she wasn't engrossed in it; instead she was gazing unseeingly into the distance.

'Hi,' he said.

She jumped, the book falling from her hands. 'Deangelo? What are you doing here?'

'I came to tell you that you were right. That revenge is no substitution for living. And I came to give you this.' He handed over the large gift bag he carried and she took it in shaking hands but made no move to look inside.

'You already gave me so much.'

'This is different.'

She held his gaze uncertainly before opening the bag and peeking inside.

It was a rose. One perfect white rose. The most perfect rose sold at New Covent Garden that day.

Harriet's hands shook as she drew the rose carefully out of the bag, appreciating the charm of the delicate crystal bud vase, her heart swelling as she looked at it.

'You remembered?'

'When your dad asked what you wanted you asked for flowers. And he would bring you one perfect rose every Friday.'

'You do remember.' She inhaled the rich scent and looked up at Deangelo, blinking back hot tears. Tears of joy, and of an aching nostalgic sadness. 'Nobody has brought me a flower since he started to get sick. I can't tell you how much this means.'

'White roses symbolise a heart unacquainted with love,' he said ruefully. 'That was me. That rose is my heart before I met you.'

Hope, sweet and joyful, began to unfurl inside her. Still holding the rose, Harriet got to her feet and stood in front of him, carefully examining his face, every feature imprinted on her heart. There was something subtly different about his expression, the self-loathing that had always lurked behind the careful mask was gone, as was the mask itself. She'd never seen such candour in his face, nor such tenderness. 'And now?'

'And now I'd need a whole rainbow of roses to express how I feel.' He looked behind him. 'As you can see.'

Harriet stared at the sitting/dining room. A driver was carrying a huge bouquet, so big she was surprised it had fitted through the door, made up of every colour of rose imaginable.

'That's...' She couldn't find the words. 'Thank you.'

'It should be me thanking you. For everything, But for now I just wanted to give you my heart. My cold, unloving heart, if you'll have it, and to tell you that, thanks to you, it isn't cold any more. To tell you that I love you.'

The words hung there, Harriet staring up at him, searching his face for a sign that this was real, that she could believe this was really happening. All she saw was love—love for her. Love, hope and a hint of nerves, which convinced her more than any words, any gesture could that he meant it. 'Deangelo...'

'You don't have to say anything. You don't owe me anything. I just wanted you to know how I feel. To know I'm on your side, always. No matter what.'

Harriet's heart was hammering so loudly she could barely think, her chest tight with suppressed tears—tears and a joy she didn't wholly trust just yet. 'But what about Brazil? The hotels?'

'Still intact. My siblings still have their share and will still have an income—a reduced income as we need to reinvest in the hotels, but a fair one. Not that they believe that. I don't think they'd hate me any more if I had beggared them.'

'Maybe not, but you would have ended up hating yourself.'

'I was halfway there,' he confessed. 'But in the end I didn't want my choices to be born out of hate and fear, but from love and hope. I wanted to make the choices which meant I would deserve you. If you'd have me. To take the path that led me to you. I have more money than I ever dreamed, but it's not brought me one moment's peace or joy. One night with you was worth more than every penny I own. And what I'd like, what I hope you'd like, is to turn that night into a lifetime.'

'A lifetime?' Had she heard him right? Carefully, she set the rose down on the bench. 'Deangelo...' She couldn't finish the sentence, her heart too full for words.

'For several years I went to work looking for a reason to carry on, not seeing that reason was right in front of me. I don't want to waste any more time, Harriet.' And as she watched him with wondering eyes he pulled a familiar box out of his pocket. 'Last time I gave you this it was pretence. I just didn't realise I was pretending to myself, pretending I hadn't picked the perfect ring for the perfect woman. But no more pretending, Harriet. I love you and I want to spend my life with you. If you'll have me.'

She noticed his hands were shaking as he handed her the box, and she opened it to see just the sapphire ring on its bed of white satin.

'The other ring is safe, waiting for the day you do me the honour of becoming my wife. If you will, that is. Will you, Harriet? Will you marry me?'

Harriet stepped close and took his hand in hers. 'Yes. And not because of the perfect ring or the fancy suits or the money. None of that means anything to me. But because you saw me. Because you took care of me. And because I want to take care of you. I love you, Deangelo Santos. So yes.'

She gave him the ring box back, holding out her hand and, with unusually clumsy fingers, he placed the ring on her finger, where it belonged.

'I should have come back with you when you asked,' he said. 'Shouldn't have let my life be governed by fear. Fear of losing people I loved, fear of letting them down, of being unworthy. But in the end I realised that the only thing worse than losing you would be never having you at all.'

'I'm right here,' she vowed. 'I'm not going anywhere. I don't know what the future holds—you and I both know how precarious happiness can be. But I can promise you that I won't hide any more. That I am going to love each day and wring every moment of happiness from life that I can. And there is no one else I want to do that with.'

This was where she belonged—wherever Deangelo was. She smiled up at him, filled with happiness and the sweetness of hope. The tenderness in his eyes nearly undid her as he gently tilted her chin, leaning in to kiss her, and Harriet knew that, whatever obstacles the future held, neither of them would ever know loneliness again.

* * * * *

*Look out for the next story in
the Fairytale Brides quartet
Coming soon!*

*And if you enjoyed this story,
check out these other great reads
from Jessica Gilmore*

Summer Romance with the Italian Tycoon
Baby Surprise for the Spanish Billionaire
The Sheikh's Pregnant Bride
A Proposal from the Crown Prince

All available now!